BARSET
REVISITED

Ronald McGowan

Pen Press Publishers

First published in Great Britain by
Pen Press Publishers Ltd
25 Eastern Place
Brighton BN2 1GJ

ISBN 978-1-906206-90-1

Printed and bound in the UK

A catalogue record of this book is available from
the British Library

Cover design by Jacqueline Abromeit

BARSET
REVISITED

Chapter One

COSBY LODGE

Breakfast at Cosby Lodge, since Major Grantly's marriage, was a far cry from the solitary bite of his bachelor days. Indeed, the breakfast room would not have been recognised as the old gunroom where the major used to take his quick repast before setting out for a morning's sport. Gone were the rods and guns, the bags and boots that used to fill the space, and in their place were silver and china, chintzes and tablecloths and all the appurtenances of a full, feminine state breakfast. Where the bachelor's rods had stood on their rack, now shone the married man's sideboard, its array of silver warming dishes winking in the morning light. Where the air had once told of gunpowder and tobacco it was now scented with tea and coffee, and all was mahogany and lace where once there was oak and steel.

The Major told himself that this was good and that he was fortunate indeed to have been blessed with such a wife. He told himself so daily, and with such success that it was a rare morning when he even considered the possibility that he might be wrong. How different he was in this from other men of his generation I will leave for the reader to decide.

In any case, today was not such a morning. He looked up from the post with the true Grantly smile on his face.

"Well, Grace, here is some news at last. It is from my father. His trip to London has borne fruit this time. They have made him Bishop of Westminster after all. You will recall it was promised to him some years ago, but the ministry fell and the new men would have none of him. Now our friends are in again and he is to have his mitre at last."

Mrs. Grantly's recollection of a promise which had been broken when she was still at her copybook was somewhat less than accurate, but she made it a practice always to support her husband in his declarations, so she merely continued pouring the Lapsang Souchong as she replied.

"What good news my dear. Of course I did not know your dear father at the time, but I am sure he was greatly disappointed when old Bishop Grantly died. I rejoice for him now."

The death of Major Grantly's grandfather had occasioned expectations of the see of Barchester. The offer of that of Westminster had come some years later, and it pained Major Grantly to realise that his wife was still not completely au fait with the history of the illustrious family she had joined. This was not the time and place to attempt to cure that fault, however.

"There is more, my love, and more cause for rejoicing too. It is about your father."

"Poor, dear father. I sometimes think he is too, too good for this wicked world. Even now, when he could afford a new coat now and then, and new soles for his boots, and the odd coat of paint on his walls, he never thinks of anything but his studies and sermons. Why, only the other day....."

"Yes, dear, we all admire your father's learning greatly, but what I wish to say is that the archdeacon – the bishop, we should say – regrets greatly that his translation will mean the severance of many connections – many very old connections –with Barsetshire. He regrets it the more as both he and his father before him have been such notable personages in the county for so long. There are many old friends he fears he will no longer be able to see with the frequency he would desire, many other things he fears he will no longer have time for.

These partings are inevitable, however. As Bishop of Westminster he cannot remain as archdeacon of Barset. He regrets that he will have no say in the matter of his successor, but rejoices that at least it will not be left completely to Bishop Proudie. "

Here Major Grantly's attention wandered for a while as he contemplated the almost lifelong war that had been waged in Barset by the Grantlys, with their allies the Luftons and the Arabins against the Proudies. He could barely remember Mrs. Proudie, who had started it all, or at least turned an armed neutrality towards the man who had usurped the Grantly bishopric into outright war. She had died when he was quite a boy, but the feud had rumbled on these twenty years. Whatever would the gossips of Barchester think of to talk about now?

He was recalled to the present by a fresh cup, and his wife's words as she handed it.

"The dear archdeacon – that is to say, the bishop – would never forget a friend, I am sure. "

"Just so, my love, and although he has no influence over who is to be the next archdeacon, there is one appointment which is in his gift."

"If he proposes to ask father to be his chaplain, I doubt if we will be able to persuade him. Saint Ewold's parish may seem a small thing to a bishop, or even to an archdeacon, but I assure you that after the poverty in which we lived before your grandfather, that good, kind, sainted man, took pity on us......."

The good, kind, sainted man in question was the Reverend Septimus Harding, Major Grantly's maternal grandfather, and while the Major retained loving memories of an indulgent old man, he also could not help thinking of him as ....not quite a Grantly.

"Yes, yes, my dear, we need not go into all that. My father has the greatest respect for yours, both as a Christian, as a scholar, as a man of the cloth, and as a gentleman. He would never think of insulting him by offering him a chaplaincy. No, he has rather more than that in mind. He does not consider that his Episcopal duties will permit him to attend to his parish as he would wish. I believe there are precedents, but pluralism is so frowned upon these days, and the idea of a perpetual curate has always been particularly repugnant to my father. He is consequently resigning as Rector of Plumstead."

"But surely he cannot think that Bishop Proudie will give Plumstead to any but one of his creatures?"

"I do not think the poor Bishop is half as black as my father would paint him. But in this case he will not be permitted to display whatever negritude he may possess. Bishop Proudie has nothing to do in this matter. My father, remember, is squire of Plumstead as well as Rector. The living is in his gift, and he wishes to bestow it upon Mr. Crawley."

"Oh! But the archdeacon – that is to say, his grace – is too good. And think how my father will feel at this further benevolence from your family."

"My dear, say rather, 'From our family.' But what my father wishes to know is whether Mr. Crawley will accept the offer. We all have the very greatest respect for your father, but you must admit that he can sometimes appear quite....well, quite....whimsical."

"Oh dear,"Grace sighed. It had been said, and she could not deny it.

Chapter Two

MR. CRAWLEY

Those who have followed the history of Barsetshire will need no reminding of the famous court case in which the Reverend Josiah Crawley, the perpetual curate of Hogglestock, was accused of fraudulently cashing a cheque for twenty pounds.

They will also need no reminding of how the entire Grantly faction and all its ramifications – the Thornes, the Arabins, the Dales and the Luftons had rallied round and how Mr. Crawley had been saved in the end by the combined efforts of Mrs. Arabin and a young cousin of the Crawleys called Johnny Eames. Indeed, young Mr. Eames had exerted himself greatly in the matter for a particular reason – a particular reason apart from his relationship, that is - and it had always seemed to those who knew the ins and outs of the case that it was a great shame when he had not received the obvious reward for his efforts. But this is by the way.

Mr. Crawley's "whimsicality" would be called "obstinacy" by some and by others "integrity". It consisted chiefly of a conviction that he himself was the only judge of his conduct and that the opinion of the world was in no sense to be his guide. That is not to say that Mr. Crawley set out to flout the world's opinion. Far from it. The opinion of the world –that is to say, the world as he saw it- was something by which Mr. Crawley set great store. But his world was a purely clerical one, and a narrow one at that, consisting chiefly of his own family and their connections, the Arabins and Grantlys. Bishop Proudie he had had dealings with in the past, and thought him an ambitious, worldly man whose notions were not to be considered by anyone desirous of saving his soul. Mr. Crawley was extremely desirous of saving his soul. He wished, nay, longed -with all his heart - to do right, but he was often sorely puzzled as to where that right was to be found.

It was by no means to be taken for granted that he would consider a promotion which would enable him and his family to live in comfort for the rest of their lives as being "right" in his own sense. He was just as likely to consider that he could not leave Saint Ewolds out of obligation to his parishioners, or to Mr. Harding who had resigned him the living, or for any one of a hundred other reasons which would never occur to those of a less original turn of mind.

For it cannot be doubted that, from a worldly point of view, Plumstead was a far greater prize than St. Ewold's. The latter, a small parish just outside the city of Barchester, barely yielded its incumbent two hundred pounds a year and a tiny, almost rundown vicarage. Old Mr. Harding, who latterly resided with his daughter in Barchester, had never used the house and so was unaware of its shortcomings. Mr. Crawley, however, could not help but be conscious of its inadequacies as the home for a family man. Had he been inclined to forget them, his wife would have made sure that he did not.

Plumstead, on the other hand had a guaranteed stipend of £1200 a year and a large, almost palatial rectory with grounds to match. It was regarded as among the most succulent of the plums in the diocese of Barchester, and many were the prebends and rural vicars who would have done wonders to obtain it. The rector of Plumstead, too, was a much more substantial personage in the diocese than any curate of Hogglestock or vicar of St. Ewold's could ever be. Men would not forget that the last two incumbents had gone on to become Archdeacons and even Bishops at last. Mr. Crawley himself was singularly without ambition, but Mrs. Crawley, with a daughter still to marry, was not above such considerations.

Wherefore Grace sighed, and said,
"Oh dear!"

Chapter Three

WHAT WAS DECIDED AT COSBY LODGE

"Oh dear," said Grace, "I am sure he will refuse. He will think himself bound to the memory of Mr. Harding, or to his parishioners. Either that or he will recollect a dozen other cases more deserving than he . And I know my mother would be so pleased."

Major Grantly allowed a frown to mar the serenity of his brow.

"And what of the offence a refusal would give to my father, my dear? It is not every day that such offers are made. And who knows what other gifts a bishop may have in the future?"

This discussion might have continued all morning, for the Major was a gentleman who took the honour of his family quite seriously, and one, moreover, who had absolutely nothing to do that morning save indulge in the delights of a mild family quarrel. It was interrupted, however, by the entry of the nurserymaid with the news that young Master Henry was fretting and hot and seemed to be poorly.

This domestic emergency took absolute precedence and resulted in the summoning of Doctor Crofts from Barchester.

The servant despatched with the message had the good fortune to find the doctor at home. Dr. Crofts called at Cosby Lodge within the hour of his summoning, and dealt with the infantile ailment with his usual good sense. Having prescribed the necessary palliative, he assured the parents that there was no cause for any alarm at all.

"These things blow up so quickly in children of that age, and in ninety nine cases out of a hundred they blow over just as quickly. It is nothing more than over-excitement, and possibly an excessive indulgence in sugarplums. If he is no better by the morning, by all means send for me."

The fond parents were only too eager to be reassured, and so great was their confidence in their physician that, with the child in his safe hands, they had even been able to return their thoughts to the problem of the morning. The beginnings of a plan had occurred to Grace's mind, and she whispered it discreetly to her husband, who acted upon it with the despatch which had won him his reputation in the light dragoons.

"By the by, Crofts, please do us the honour of coming to dinner on Saturday, with Mrs. Crofts and her sister, of course. There will be only a few friends, and I would particularly like to discuss something with you then."

"Would this something be professional?"

"No, no. Not at all. It concerns my father in law and how we can do some good to him, which, as you know, is not easy to accomplish."

And Major Grantly unfolded the situation to the doctor, with the result that the latter promised to call on certain friends before the Saturday and to see what could be done towards concerting their actions.

Chapter Four

A SICKLY SEASON IN BARCHESTER

The practice of Doctor Crofts in the city of Barchester was much patronised by the clergy of that city and the surrounding area, in spite of the fact that the doctor had not long removed there from Guestwick. The reasons for his popularity had much to do with his having taken over the practice of one Doctor Filgrave, who had, previous to his retirement, the care of much of the Barchester establishment in his hands, and even more to do with Doctor Croft's connections, in that having married a young lady of very little fortune but very good family did him no harm in the eyes of his patients. These patients looked above all in their physicians for a gentlemanlike manner and easy conversation. Some medical ability was an advantage, to be sure, but Barchester was a cathedral city and its citizenry knew full well not to expect miracles. Indeed Doctor Crofts' professional skill was not generally appreciated outside his profession, where he was known to be one of the leading lights of that limited world. The world of Barchester, however, cared more for his Dale relatives and his long friendship with Earl De Guest than for all his diplomas.

For Mrs. Crofts, of course, had been Miss. Isabella Dale before her marriage, and was still reckoned part of county society. Such a thing it still is in England, to have an uncle the lord of the manor in which you are dwelling and a great uncle an earl in the neighbouring parish.

Now Mrs. Crofts had a sister, younger by two years, who was living with her. Some years past now, Miss Lily Dale had had a misfortune. Those familiar with the ways of Barsetshire will also be familiar with that misfortune, but for those not so well-versed, there is no short way to put it but to say that she had been – jilted. That is to say, a young man, named Adolphus Crosbie had proposed to her, been accepted, and then decided he could do better with an earl's daughter than an earl's great-niece. Whether this was also a misfortune for the Lady Alexandrina de Courcy whom he eventually led to the altar has been a matter of some dispute. The lady finally found it so, and the gentleman –if gentleman he may be called – came at last to agree with her as to the unsuitability of the match. But that is another story, which has been told elsewhere.

Miss Dale herself had borne up well under her misfortune – or so it seemed to the world. There had been no pining, no decline, very little weeping. Indeed, the world had thought her very likely to console herself with another admirer, an unexceptionable young man who was also rather a favourite with most of her family. When this young man took it upon himself to chastise Mr. Crosbie after Miss Dale's only male relative of a suitable age had declined to do so, all concerned thought the match to be very probable.

Almost all concerned, that is. The two most concerned of all did not happen to agree with the world, the young man from natural diffidence, and the young lady from a certain conviction that "The Dales were ever constant", and, having once given her word to one man, it was beneath her ever to consider another. So it had transpired that Miss Lily Dale was still Miss Lily Dale, and now living with her sister in Barchester.

Chapter Five

CHANGES AT ALLINGTON

That Miss Dale was not still living in the Small House at Allington, which might almost be considered the ancestral home of the cadet branch of the Dale family, came about thus.

After the events referred to above, and the much happier one of her sister's marriage, it appeared that although Miss Dale herself refused to indulge in the expected decline, her nearest and dearest felt obliged to do so on her behalf. The first to follow this course was her Uncle Christopher, Dale of Allington himself. His declining years he had devoted to two projects – the marriage of his niece Isabella to her cousin Bernard, and that of his niece Lily to a very deserving young man who had been her childhood sweetheart. The frustration of both these projects left him with nothing to live for, and Mrs. Crofts' bridal white was very soon followed by the assumption of black for her uncle.

This had naturally occasioned many changes at Allington.

Mr. Bernard Dale, the heir to the property, was a military gentleman, recently become a widower,and much sought after at the Horse

Guards. Memories of his wife, an excellent lady, a niece of Mrs. Thorne of Chaldicotes, who had brought him twenty thousand pounds on the marriage, at first rendered him not much inclined to spending time on the affairs of the estate. But not many months after he succeeded to the property there was an alteration in his circumstances which made the life of a country gentleman seem more desirable. One of his associates in the capital introduced him to a young lady. The young lady was as fair as young ladies generally are. She was amenable, in so far as young ladies generally are amenable to the attentions of eligible young men. She was very much in his way. She was, unfortunately, American. This was very much a handicap but nowadays such handicaps are apt to be outweighed by other considerations, and all the world agreed in setting her down as enormously rich.

That is to say, her father was rich. Miss Arabella Kornhopper was the only child of Mr. Otis P. Kornhopper, of Kornhopper's Kentucky Ketchup. Mr. Kornhopper had made an indeterminate number of millions from the sale throughout the Eastern Seaboard of a lurid red fluid which had some success in adding flavour of a sort back to food from which the American cooking process had carefully extracted the last vestiges of taste. He had done so by himself extracting all vestiges of taste from his advertising, and posters and placards all over the States extolled the virtues of KKK and exhorted the public to buy it in terms which would have made an English costermonger wince.

Bernard Dale met Miss Kornhopper at a party in London. The acquaintance progressed as such acquaintances generally do, with the result that before very long it became known to the world that Mr. Dale and Miss Kornhopper were engaged to be married.

At this point it became necessary to deal with Mr. Kornhopper, and to introduce the prospective bride to her future home at Allington. The effusive rapture with which Miss Kornhopper greeted the Great House may be imagined, and was not entirely unexpected by her betrothed. But what came as a surprise to all was the reaction of her father to the village and its surroundings.

There was much discussion at the Small House the morning after.

"Isn't he just a darling?" said Lily. "I could not believe anyone could be so like the "Domestic Manners". And the way he exclaimed about everything! " Yuh don' say, Mr. Dale? This house wuz built in King James's tahme? The King James as writ the bahble? Waal Ah'll be...""

"Lily, you wicked girl!" exclaimed her mother. "Mr. Kornhopper is a .....well, I don't know just what to say about him, but you should not mock him like that. Especially as here is Bernard come to tell us all about his plans for the day."

For the figure of Bernard could be seen through the window as he crossed the bridge leading from the garden of the Great House.

It was, of course, necessary to welcome him and provide him with tea before he could be interrogated as to his guests, of whom he seemed strangely reluctant to speak.

"Well," said Lily, "what do our American cousins intend to do today? Will they buy Guestwick, or will Allington be enough for them? Or will they merely languish in the country air and think romantic thoughts about the mother country?"

"Don't jest, Lily," replied Bernard. "Your shots are getting all too near the mark. Miss Kornhopper and Mr. Kornhopper will probably return to London today, and I cannot say when, or, indeed, if they will be seen in Allington again. Things were said between Mr. Kornhopper and myself last night which make it seem unlikely that the marriage will proceed."

"Surely not," said Mrs. Dale. "I thought all was settled bar the date."

Bernard shrugged. There are shrugs which indicate indifference and shrugs which signify ignorance. There are shrugs which show the scorn of the shrugger and others which are merely habitual. This was none of those. If anything, it seemed to say that the subject was out of the hands of all present, nothing could be done about it. Bernard shrugged, then, and at length seemed to make up his mind.

"Mr. Kornhopper is putting forward conditions for his consent. Conditions which seem reasonable to himself but which cannot possibly be met. The thing is, he wants to buy the Small House."

"Buy the Small House! Impossible!"

"Exactly. But I should be greatly obliged if anyone could tell me how to explain that to an American."

"But why should he want to buy the Small House

of all places? He could have the grandest house in England – or America or anywhere else. What attraction has Allington for him?"

"It has his daughter- or was going to have his daughter. Like most of his countrymen, Mr. Kornhopper is, I suspect, deeply sentimental au fond. He really cannot bear to be parted from her. And, again, like many of his compatriots, he hankers after calling himself an English country gentleman. Seeing the Small House next to the Great House where his daughter will live has given him the idea that he can combine the two wishes of his heart."

"But surely he knows it cannot be?"

"I told him so, but I was sorely vexed to explain why it must be so. I told him that the property must be handed down intact and could not be alienated, and he told me to my face that he had investigated my affairs and knew that the entire estate was unencumbered and unentailed and that I could do with it as I wished. Then I reminded him that the Small House is already occupied, and after that, well, we both got rather ...enthusiastic. I should have realised, of course. He is a man of business, and an American. He thinks everything is a matter of money."

"Oh, money!" said Lily, " You naturally have no use for such an article, being a genuine English gentleman yourself. And did he name a price?"

"He said he would willingly offer me a million."

"A million? Good Heavens! Pounds or dollars?"

"Dollars, I suppose. He usually thinks and talks in dollars. But I never considered it seriously.

Things got rather excited after that, and we did not go to bed in the best of humours with each other."

"But, seriously, Bernard," said Mrs. Dale. "If he is really prepared to offer so much money, perhaps we ought to consider the subject. If he would be prepared to take a lease rather than the freehold, I am sure Lily would agree that we could not stand between you and such an amount. We have nearly moved to Guestwick once already you know. And in a way, the Small House would still be home to one of the family."

"Do you really love Miss Kornhopper so much?" asked Lily. "As much as you loved someone else a while ago?"

Bernard had at one time been a suitor for the hand of her sister Bell, and his first wife, Emily, had been one of Lily's dearest friends.

Bernard squared his shoulders.

"I love Bell dearly, as I love both of you here," he said. "I loved Emily with all my heart, but she is gone. I know you will not take it amiss if I say that I cannot bear to think of life without Arabella."

"Then marry her," said Lily. "And if it takes the Small House to bring her father round, we will find a way."

And a way was found, in the way that these things are found when marriage and property is involved. Mr. Kornhopper settled his million dollars on his daughter on her marriage, and also paid a substantial sum to the "tenants" for giving up their occupation. Somehow it was managed that those tenants should include Bell, and her share went very well towards the cost of the new Barchester practice, and the big brick house near the close, where the whole family now removed.

"For after all," said Lily, " there was nowhere for us to stay in Allington, and no-one to keep us in Guestwick, and at least in Barchester we can be near Bell and the Grantlys."

Chapter Six

DINNER AT COSBY LODGE

The candles shone brightly at Cosby Lodge the following Saturday. Their warm glow looked particularly well reflected in the glass and silver and polished mahogany of the dining room, with its crisp white linen and the warm reds and golds of the carpet.

Not for the first time, Grace wondered at her good fortune. Accustomed from youth to bare boards, and often bare tables too, she still found it marvellous that she should be mistress of all this. She could never forget Henry's goodness at that awful time when everything and everyone had seemed against her family.

Not quite everyone, she corrected herself, with that strict regard for truth which had been bred into her. There had been some, apart from Henry, who had stood by the Crawleys. The Robartses had been true, and the Luftons and the Thornes. Mark Robarts had stood bail for her father, and Lord Lufton and Doctor Thorne, although compelled as magistrates to commit Mr. Crawley for trial, had done so most reluctantly.

The Dales had been true, too. At that time, Lily Dale had been Grace's closest friend outside her family, and she had been the first to proclaim her belief in Mr. Crawley's innocence before the world. Lily Dale at that time had been something of an idol to Grace, her ideal of what a young lady should be. Time had passed, and Lily Dale at twenty-eight no longer seemed so grand and romantic to Grace at twenty-three as she had when their ages were twenty-three and eighteen. They were still the best of friends, but the wife and mother could not feel quite the same towards someone who seemed set to be an old maid.

Grace had not given so many dinner parties of her own as to be past feeling the excitement of anticipation. This evening was to be a success, and it was to be particularly so because of the purpose behind it. If there was any way in which the concerted efforts of all his friends could effect it, Mr. Crawley's fortune was to be made in spite of himself.

The Crofts party arrived in good time.

They had been particularly requested to do so by Mrs. Grantly for a purpose of her own. To that end she took Miss Dale aside shortly after they had arrived.

"Dear Lily, I do wish you would give me some advice. We all think so highly of your understanding, especially my dear father, that I believe you will certainly be able to help us."

And so she set forth the whole thorny problem, of how Mr. Crawley was to be persuaded to accept what would be only to his own good in spite of any doubts he might have about such unaccustomed good fortune.

Now Miss Dale was a particular favourite of Mr. Crawley, whose church she had attended since her first day in Barchester, and she had already been made acquainted with the circumstances of the case by her sister's husband, who was inclined to treat the vicar of St. Ewold's as an interesting medical case. She had had her own thoughts on the best way to approach the reluctant clergyman, and she opened her mind to her friend.

By deliberate consent, the other guests also arrived before Mr. Crawley, and so had time to consult each other.

So it was that when all sat down to dinner, all save the unsuspecting victim knew what was in store.

While the ladies were present every subject was discussed except that which was in the minds of most of those in the room. Mr. Crawley was artfully seated between Lily and young Lady Lufton, whom he remembered very fondly as Lucy Robarts. These ladies might be said to be those outside his own family whom he valued most in the world. That they were still, in his eyes, young ladies did no harm at all to their wicked purpose, which was simply to charm him and get him into a suitable mood for the gentlemen to begin their work.

When the ladies had retired, the gentlemen grouped themselves for their battle. The lines had been laid out and the positions assigned by their military adviser, although the plan had been generally agreed. That it would be a battle, none had any doubt. To get Mr. Crawley to agree to do what was good for him was a task which had seldom met with success in the past.

The opening shot was fired by Doctor Thorne, so as to allay any suspicion of deliberate clerical manoeuverings.

"What's this I hear, Grantly, about your father being to be congratulated?"

"What, have you heard already? How the news does travel! We only heard ourselves the other day. Yes, it has come his way at last. By the end of next month he will be Bishop of Westminster, with his own mitre and crozier and whatever else bishops do have."

"Then at least Westminster will have a gentleman for a bishop," put in Lord Lufton. "unlike some sees I could name. But it's a long time to the end of next month. What if the ministry should fall? I remember how cut up he was last time he was disappointed that way. It would be like to break his heart if it happened again."

"It would indeed. But I will tell you something else that seems likely to break his heart, even if the ministry does not change, and that is leaving Plumstead. After all, my father has been Archdeacon of Barchester for forty years now, so much so that none of us can think of him as anything else. But he has been Rector of Plumstead for even longer."

"But surely," said Mark Robarts. "Surely the preferment will take away the sting."

"There speaks the ambitious cleric." laughed the Major. "And you are right, of course. What I should have said is that it would break his heart to leave Plumstead in the wrong hands. He cannot bear the thought of his own parish – for he thinks of

Plumstead as belonging to him – falling prey to an innovator, a moderniser, who would perhaps turn the church into some parody of Messrs. Moody and Sankey. What would really ease his mind would be the knowledge that the living would go to someone of whom he approves, a gentleman of taste and education, and of the right way of thinking as to matters clerical."

So the conversation went on, everything said tending to the conclusion that it would be a kindness to Bishop Grantly to find a new incumbent for his old parish.

At last Lord Lufton took the bull by the horns.

"Would not you consider moving to Plumstead, Mr. Crawley? I am sure that we would all be very pleased to see you there."

"I am flattered, my lord, that you should deem me worthy of such a position, but I assure you that I am very content with my present situation."

"So am I," put in Robarts "I would not move from Framley for anything less than a bishop's hat myself. But were I at St. Ewolds and Plumstead were offered to me I should not hesitate. Come, man. Plumstead, if I may be forgiven for saying so, is the plum of the diocese, the richest living in the county. It must be twice, thrice the money."

"And is a priest to regulate his conduct according to money? I did not expect to hear such arguments from you, Mr. Robarts."

"Of course a priest is not to regulate his conduct according to money. But no one expects whoever takes over Plumstead to change his conduct in any way. That is why it is so important to have the right man."

"My father," said Major Grantly at this point, "has mentioned to me that he would be very glad to see Mr. Crawley at Plumstead Rectory."

"Your father," said Mr. Crawley, "is very kind. All your family have been very kind to me and mine. That is precisely the reason why I should be averse to accept any further kindness from them."

"But come, we are all one family now. If members of the same family cannot help each other, who can?"

So the talk went on, and by the time they joined the ladies, Mr. Crawley had admitted that he could fill the post at Plumstead satisfactorily, but maintained that it was out of the question for him to leave St. Ewolds.

This was as much success as anyone had expected. Now it was time for the second line of attack.

Lily brought Mr. Crawley his tea, and sat down beside him.

"And what have you gentlemen been talking about over your port?" she asked.

"The gentlemen," said Mr. Crawley, have been attempting to persuade me that I should accept further charity from Major Grantly's father. Their intentions, I have no doubt, are only of the best, but I fear that I must decline to increase my already too great indebtedness to the family of my daughter's husband. I remember only too well what it is to be an object of charity, and my present circumstances are comparatively easy only because of the eleemosynary benevolence of the good Mr. Harding. Loth as I am to give offence, I can consent to no further alms."

"Well, Mr. Crawley, of course it is not for me to advise you. But have you considered that perhaps the charity would be flowing the other way in this case? Grace has spoken to me about the letter they received from the old archdeacon, and I gather he is terribly worried that some creature of Bishop Proudie's should obtain the preferment. Living as we are right next to the close in Barchester, we hear these things, you know, and I have heard it said that the bishop has Mr. Thumble in mind for the position."

Now Mr. Crawley had crossed swords with Bishop Proudie on several occasions in the past, and with Mr. Thumble even more times. Of neither of them did he have the slightest opinion, and from this time he began to wonder whether it might not after all be for the best if he should go to Plumstead rectory.

"That may be as you say, Miss Dale, and while I thank you for the kind interest you have taken in my affairs, I cannot but remember that I have an obligation to my present parish. I also have an obligation to the archdeacon, who was so kind as to present me to it."

"But now it is the archdeacon who wishes you to give it up. Could you not oblige him in a way which would also do your family so much good? And as for St. Ewolds, surely there would be nothing to prevent you employing a curate. And think what a position that would be for your Charles. You were saying earlier that he is at a loss what to do for a living after he comes down from Oxford."

Now Mr. Crawley was an unusual man, but he was human. He had spent the greater part of his working life as a perpetual curate, and the thought of having a curate of his own had a peculiar attraction for him. The thought of being also able to provide for his own son, whose career at Marlborough and Oxford had been so far dependent upon the charity of Dean Arabin was also far from uncongenial.

"I will think upon what you have said, young lady," he said.

And by the end of the evening, he had so far been worked upon as to consider that it might after all be not impossible for the Reverend Josiah Crawley to become Rector of Plumstead Episcopi.

By the following morning, when the Major begged an interview of him before his departure, and broached the subject in form, he had so far persuaded himself that he was able to accept with a show of graciousness that surprised all.

"Miss Dale," said the Major to Grace afterwards, "has worked wonders."

"It is no more than I expected of Lily," said Grace. "She always did."

Chapter Seven

PROFESSIONAL FAME

It has been said that the practice of Doctor Crofts in Barchester was known particularly for its gentlemanliness rather than its professional skill, and that this did the good doctor no harm with his patients. The world of Barchester knew him as a well-bred, conversable young man, with pleasant manners, who could be trusted to act discreetly, and whose patients died no more often than anyone else's. The world of Barchester thought this sufficient, but there was a greater world outside Barchester, and it thought rather differently of Doctor Crofts.

Indeed, his name appeared very often on learned articles in the Lancet, he had been corresponding with Doctor Snow on the treatment of typhoid fever, and the medical world had become greatly excited about some of his proposals. It had become so excited that a few mornings after the Crofts' return from Cosby, a letter arrived with an invitation to address the Royal College of Physicians the following month.

Dr. and Mrs. Crofts took the news in different ways. The doctor was both flattered and perturbed.

Convinced though he was that his methods were the path to the true cure for the disease, he could not relish the thought of standing on his legs for an hour or more before an audience of his peers, all ready to demolish him in an instant. Mrs. Crofts, however, had no such fears. This recognition was just what her husband deserved, and could only be the first step on the road to the medical knighthood which he deserved even more. She would hear of nothing but immediate acceptance. The questions of providing for the doctor's patients and maintaining his household in his absence might all be settled later. But now he must seize this opportunity.

On the same day, a letter came for Lily. She read it after breakfast and lost no time in speaking of it to her mother and sister.

"The Grantlys are going up to London next week to visit the Bishop. They will probably stay for the rest of the season. Grace asks me to go with her, but of course I shall decline. I could not possibly spend so long away from you all, and I have been to London already, you know."

"But, Lily, that would be just perfect. I realise that you do not wish to impose on the Grantlys for so long, but it would just fit so nicely. If you stay with them for a month, you can come to us after that, and we can all have another month together in town, for we shall be there by then."

And she explained their plans, and implored Lily's compliance.

"I have not had a season in London, like you, you know, but I am sure I shall not know what to do with myself while Charles is shut up with all his medical bigwigs all day. And, Lily, you are not getting any younger, you know."

By which she meant to signify that there was still a chance of fishing for a husband in the bigger pond of the metropolis.

Lily understood this perfectly.

"I see you are still set on not having an old maid in the family. It will not do, but I suppose I shall have to humour you. But who will look after the house and the children if we are all in London?"

"I will," said Mrs. Dale. "I have no wish to go to London, and there are one or two things I want to do which can be done more easily with the house empty. You young people will enjoy yourselves far more without me to spoil things for you."

Mrs. Dale remained deaf to all protests that the trip would not be the same without her and that her elder daughter was an old married woman too. She knew quite well that she would not go, and so did her daughters.

Lily replied to Mrs. Grantly that very afternoon.

"My dear Grace," she wrote, *"I thank you with all my heart for your kind invitation, and shall be delighted to accept, the more so as Bell and Charles will be taking rooms in London in a month's time and I will not need to impose upon you for so very long. Please do not expect me to have any grand acquaintances to introduce to you. My time in London was spent almost entirely with my uncle and Mrs. Thorne, who, of course, knew everybody. You might think it a delicate matter meeting friends of Emily Dunstable now that Bernard has remarried. But I*

do look forward to making the acquaintance of your father in law.

"I shall be with you on Wednesday, and promise to work my passage industriously for as long as it pleases you to put up with me."

Chapter Eight

THE BISHOP OF WESTMINSTER

The right reverend Theophilus Grantly, D.D., sometime archdeacon of Barchester and now bishop of Westminster, was a man who had often been accused of ambition. The son of a bishop himself, the holder for many years of the highest position, next to the episcopate , in his own father's diocese, there were also not wanting those who found that he cared only for feathering his own nest, and that things of this world weighed much more with him than those of the next.

It need hardly be said that those who thought thus were guilty of a vile traduction of Doctor Grantly's true character. He was a man who appreciated the good things of life, and whose life had afforded him many opportunities to exercise that appreciation. His father had been bishop of Barchester at a time when to be bishop of Barchester was worth something. That he should choose his own son as his archdeacon was, perhaps, nepotistic in the strictest sense, but none had ever been able to claim with justification that the diocese had in any way suffered under the regime of father and son. Not even Mrs. Proudie in the bitterest days of the conflict in Barchester had been able to find grounds for just complaint against the archdeacon, nor had his detractors (and they had not been lacking) succeeded in putting forward the name of another candidate who might have filled the post more satisfactorily.

Doctor Grantly was a sociable man and a gentleman, learned enough and devout enough for his profession, but not so excessively so as to make laymen find him uncongenial. His kind hospitality had won him many solid, reliable friends, but his frankness and hatred of the canting hypocrisy so lately popular among the cloth had also furnished him many solid, reliable enemies.

Still, those who derided him and called him worldly did him an injustice. Whatever else he might be, Dr. Grantly was a devout Christian, and a devoted pillar of the church of England. His opinions as to the way that church should be regulated and conducted might not be entirely in accord with the current fashions, but was that necessarily a bad thing? There were many in Barsetshire who thought that it was not, and for almost a generation the archdeacon had been their champion.

Now he had lived long enough to see a time when the powers of the land – and of the church – were coming once again to realise the worth of reasonableness and civility in the place of enthusiasm and zealotry.

"For, after all," the new bishop had told the prime minister himself, "I see no reason why a clergyman should not also be a gentleman, and why those of us who wish to worship god in the way our fathers did, and their fathers before them, should not continue to do so. There is a place, to be sure, for innovation, and for ardour, but that place is not in the church, and still less in the pulpit or the cathedral."

The prime minister had quite agreed with him, adding however, that reform was another matter.

"Quite another matter," Doctor Grantly had agreed, while privately determining to avoid the subject on all future occasions.

He had been disappointed twice already in this matter of his mitre. When his father had died, everyone around him had expected that he would be the next bishop of Barchester. He had joined in that expectation, and had been bitterly frustrated when the timing of the old man's death had robbed him of the patronage on which he had relied. Then there had been the affair of the previous proposal for a new see of Westminster. In its own way, that had been even more vexatious, for promises had been made and expense of time, spirit and money had been incurred, and all in vain. There was to be no mistake about this third time, and it was with an inward sigh of relief that Doctor Grantly first put on cope and mitre, and felt the hands of the archbishop on his head.

The Grantlys, he could not help thinking, were at last back in their rightful place, in the first ranks of the Church of England.

Chapter Nine

A MODERN EPISCOPAL PALACE

His grace the Bishop of Westminster was, as has been shown, a somewhat singular prelate. He had a see, but no diocese, a cathedra but no cathedral, a mitre but no palace in which to lay it down with his crozier of an evening.

The question of the diocese – of its geography, as it were - was almost entirely political, with many committees being involved and much consultation needed. The bishop himself was only one of those consulted, and many were the interests involved. A prince of the church he might be, but one whose principality had yet to be delimited, and considering that that principality was to be carved out of the centre of the richest and most populous city in the world, it was hardly surprising that this should be so. Westminster itself must be in it, of course, but my lord Cantuar's residence at Lambeth made it necessary that the river should be the southern boundary, and Temple Bar with the domains of his brother Londiniensis equally set the eastern limits. But to the north and the west there was room for dispute, and much dispute there was. Bishop Grantly was determined that his new see should be one with tone, should be a diocese fit for a gentleman. Many, however, were the local aldermen, the landlords, and even the members of the upper and lower houses who had their own thoughts – thoughts which did not always agree with the bishop's ideas. Parishes came and went from day to day, some of them, it had to be said, no great loss. Mayfair, St. James's and Belgravia were very welcome adherents to the bishop's patrimony, while Marylebone, Bayswater and St. John's Wood were scarcely less so, and Pimlico and Victoria could hardly be avoided. But the exact boundaries in the region of Paddington and the neighbourhood of Fitzroy Square, and the desirability of areas such as Covent Garden and Soho were still occasioning much profitable work for the legal profession and bade fair to do so for many years yet.

The question of the cathedral was both more and less vexing.

"Of course, you will have the Abbey." the minister of the crown had said when offering Archdeacon Grantly the post.

But it appeared that the Abbey was one thing that Bishop Grantly certainly would not have. The Dean and Chapter had produced so many old charters, had raised so many questions of Royal peculiars and private interests, all to the upshot that although Westminster Abbey might be in the Diocese of Westminster, it was not of it, and answerable to none but the Archbishop of Canterbury.

Archdeacon Grantly had grown old measuring

the strengths of Deans and Chapters at Barchester, and Bishop Grantly knew when he was outgunned and outmanoeuvred, and when it behoved him to retire gracefully. He let it be announced that the construction of a new cathedral would be considered, and invited plans to be submitted by any architect desirous of the commission. Then he sat back to ignore the pleas for a monumental edifice of the Gothic style, or of the Classic style, or of no style at all, while he looked about for something that would suit him.

All his life had been spent in the shadow of the Norman cloisters of Barchester, in a see that dated back to before the conquest, and he found that there was to his mind something nonsensical about attempting so grandiose a pile for a brand new diocese. There were any number of perfectly good churches in his diocese, of noble proportions and hallowed history, which would not disgrace the title of cathedral. He rather thought that St. James's would do very nicely, or St. George's if the other were thought too small. St. Martin's was rather too vulgar, sticking out onto Trafalgar Square as it did, but either of the others would be very acceptable. There could be no objections on point of size, since they were adequate for their regular congregations, and for state occasions there would always be the Abbey.

For, after all, a cathedral was only of secondary importance. Bishop Grantly was old in the ways of Deans and Chapters, and knew that the less a Bishop had to do with them the better. It was not, he knew in the naves and chancels of a metropolitan church that the business of a Bishopric was done, but in the chambers of the episcopal palace.

Here, too, he was beset with plans and designs from all the best architects, but adhered firmly to ideas of his own. What need was there, for a modern bishop in a new diocese, to acquire a mediaeval pile in which to sit shivering of a winter's evening while he settled who was to be rural dean or archdeacon, and how the Sunday schools were to be conducted and all the other business of a nineteenth century bishop? That that mediaeval pile might be new from the builder's hand only made it the more unnecessary. It smacked of pretension, and the bishop had a horror of pretension. His diocese might be new, but never let it be said that it was nouveau riche or parvenu. Something more modest would be just the thing.

There were, however, bounds to modesty. Saint Patrick, when Primate of all Ireland had wielded his crozier from a turf hut, but turf huts are not at all in vogue nowadays, and a modern bishop has rather more in the way of paperwork to contend with. No, what was needed was a comfortable gentleman's residence somewhere convenient. Such a residence should be large enough to accommodate the Bishop's family together with a reasonable number of guests, and have adequate office space as well as all modern conveniences. The sort of thing inhabited by a well to do government minister, in the right spot, at a reasonable rent, would be ideal.

Fortunately, although there may be room for a

difference of opinion about the reasonableness of the rent, such buildings are not entirely unknown in the region of Mayfair, and Bishop Grantly had found just such a house in an outwardly unprepossessing street in the warren of thoroughfares between Park Lane and Curzon Square. He had taken a long lease, and furnished it anew, and set about making the acquaintance of his new neighbours. Then, feeling himself alone and cut off, as everyone does when first moving to the capital, he had started issuing invitations.

As Major Grantly's party rolled up in several cabs from the station one afternoon early in May street nothing could be seen but a high wall and an iron gate and more ironwork along the top, with a glimpse of slates and brickwork some distance behind it. After the gloom of the streets and the general dirt and bustle of the capital, Lily could not help thinking it reminded her more of a factory or a prison than a bishop's residence. Once through the gate, however, the resemblance disappeared. The carriage drive was small, to be sure, but the house was well-proportioned and cheerful enough from the outside. The very stout door was very stoutly closed, but opened at the first ring to disclose a bright hallway with a welcoming fire.

Old Doctor Grantly's welcome was equally warm. Although business had not been wanting to occupy his time, he had missed his family and his old connections in the past few months. He was not a man to fret or pine, but he found that, as he got older, he felt himself growing more and more like his father, and indeed, like his wife's father, the late Mr. Harding. He missed familiar places and familiar faces, he liked to be with people he knew were congenial, and he preferred everything to be just as it had always been. For Doctor Grantly, by now, and like his father before him, was becoming an old man.

"How good of you to come, Henry," he said, shaking hands warmly. "And dear Grace. How are the children, how are Mr. and Mrs. Crawley and dear Jane, how is everything at Plumstead? Has the magnolia flowered yet, has Mr. Thorne seen to the earths, has Mary got over her cough?"

"Really, father," replied Henry, " which of all these questions am I to answer first? Everyone at home is in the best of health.Young Henry is in his element chalking the walls of his beloved Aunt Jane. Plumstead is in good hands. There are the most important answered. As for the rest, we will talk them all through over tea. But you have forgotten to greet Miss Dale."

"Oh, yes, Miss Dale, do forgive me, how very remiss. May I say how very happy I am to welcome you here and how much I hope your stay will be both long and pleasant? My daughter-in-law has told me so much about you, and of course I knew your late uncle very well."

At this point the arrival of Mrs. Susan Grantly, serene in her new bishopessness, with the announcement that tea was served in the drawing room, cut short any further reminiscences which the bishop might have been about to make on the ancient history of the Dale family.

Over tea and crumpets, the bishop told them

all about his experiences with the architects and the politicians. Lily thought that there might have been a slight absence of matters clerical from the conversation, but this did not seem to surprise the others in any way. All agreed that St. James's would make an excellent new cathedral, so convenient and so comfortable.

"But I fear it will never be agreed," said the bishop. "All the other members of the committee will have it that it is too small. Still, I have always said that St. George's will do just as well, and it is nearly as convenient, indeed, more so for the Oxford Street shops."

"What a pity," said Lily. "Such a shame to be denied the opportunity of a modern pilgrimage to St. James's, without all the fag of going to Spain."

"No, it will never be agreed. Beware of committees, my dear. If only all politicians were more like some I could name."

"You are mixing with the grand and the mighty now, I see," said Grace. "Tell us all about the prime minister. Do you see him often."

"Oh, Mr. Gresham is all right. He and I are by way of being, if not friends, at least old acquaintances. He married Mary Thorne, you know, Doctor Thorne's niece, after she inherited who knows how many millions from Sir Roger Scatcherd. His mother was a De Courcy, of course, which explains a lot."

"I believe I remember hearing Lady Julia mention her from when she was staying at Courcy Castle," said Lily.

"Ah, dear old lady Julia. I was so sorry to hear about her. There was some mystery about her will, wasn't there, with nothing going to the new earl. I am told that things are not at all the same at Guestwick these days."

"Old Earl De Guest was a very dear friend," said Lily, "But I have never had the pleasure of meeting his heir. Indeed, I believe that the old earl had never met him either. A very distant relation, from Australia, apparently."

"Dear Griselda was often at Courcy Castle, of course. I believe it was there that she met our neighbours." And the bishop pointed towards the back of the house, in the direction of Park Lane. "Now, if only all politicians were like Mr. Palliser. Lady Glencora is something of a favourite of mine, too. I have no objection to a little originality. But you will meet them yourselves soon. They are coming to dinner tonight."

Chapter Ten

A TRADITIONAL EPISCOPAL PALACE

While his erstwhile archdeacon was enjoying the delights of the capital, back in Barchester, an old adversary was meditating a course which would astonish the world.

The right reverend Thomas Proudie, Bishop of Barchester, was a man much changed from when he first came to the diocese. Such, at least, was the opinion of the world as it went in Barsetshire. But the opinion of the world was not strictly accurate. At bottom he remained much as he always had been, a man much given to vacillation, to conciliation, to compromise, a man wishing to do good but often thwarted by circumstances. Above all he was a man who wished all about him to be happy, and was reduced to misery himself when this could not be so. There were those who said that this was because he would do anything for a quiet life. There were others who pointed out that persons addicted to idleness and self-deprecation rarely rose to the position of bishop. There were others still who put it all down to politics. Mr. Proudie's appointment had been political, no doubt about it. If the ministry had not changed at an inopportune moment, Archdeacon Grantly would have been Bishop of Barchester, rather than this interloper who had been given the preferment for his constant support of his party masters.

In a sense, all these were right, and in another sense, all were wrong. Exactly how wrong, Bishop Proudie had it in his mind to prove. He knew, none better, what was said about him. He knew that public opinion had had him firmly under he thumb of his late wife. She was, of course, an angel among women, that went without saying, and now that she was enjoying the delights of paradise there could be no question of any criticism of her. But she had been prone to – the bishop constantly sought in his mind for a less pejorative word than "interfere" or "meddle" – to....to have her own opinions about the running of the diocese and to express those opinions strongly at the most embarrassing moments. Her death had left him for a while truly desolated, but since then he had been able to proceed with his own plans for the episcopate.

Those plans had proved strangely popular. Many were the improvements which had been made to the conditions of the priesthood in his jurisdiction, to the conduct of services, to the running of Sunday Schools, to countless other details which went to ease the functioning of all connected with the Church in Barsetshire.

All this did not go entirely unnoticed. Even Archdeacon Grantly was heard to murmur that, without his devilish wife, Bishop Proudie was not so unmanageable after all.

But the diocese still remained split into two camps, the Proudyites and the Grantlyites, perpetually at war with each other over points of principle which most of them had forgotten.

To heal this split was Bishop Proudie's ambition. Not his sole ambition, however, for he was an ambitious man. Men without ambition tend, after all, to say "Nolo episcopari". Bishop Proudie knew of a certain northern diocese, which was shortly expected to be vacant, a diocese far richer than Barchester, and one moreover, which traditionally led to an archdiocese for its incumbent. It, too, was split into warring factions, and it was this to which rumour attributed the impending demise of its prelate. Who could be better qualified for such a see than the man who had ended the rift at Barchester? While archdeacon Grantly had been in the field, such healing would have been quite out of the question, but with his removal, all things were possible.

For the bishop was a politician after all, and an ambitious one too. He yet dreamed of sitting with the peers in parliament and making the laws of the land. Men had called him a mouse, but he intended to be a mouse that roared.

With this in mind he sat down one Monday morning and wrote the following letter to the rector of Framley.

"My dear Mr. Robarts,

"Would you be so kind as to call at the Palace at ten o'clock on Wednesday morning?

"I have a proposal to put to you which I think would be to our mutual advantage.

"If the suggested time is not convenient, please let me know when you would be at leisure.
"I remain, sir, your very humble servant,
Thomas Barnum."

Having penned this note he gazed on it for a while with a look of great satisfaction before ringing for the servant to take it to the post. The rest of the morning he spent in contemplating the even greater satisfaction it would be to replace the epithet "Barnum" with an even more venerable Latin title.

The receipt of this missive caused much head scratching in Framley Parsonage. The bishop had perhaps intended that this should be so, and the contemplation of Mr. Robarts' puzzlement had probably formed an ingredient to the smile which had adorned the episcopal visage as the letter left his august presence.

Mark Robarts was a man heart and soul in the Grantlyite camp. Indeed, in the absence of the old archdeacon it was a moot question whether he could not now be said to head that faction. Dean Arabin had the greater position in the diocese, but he also had more responsibilities and more business to attend to. He was, withal, a man of a temperament more scholarly than combative. Mr. Robarts had already proved himself to be capable of embarrassing his enemies, and had comparative leisure to devote to what those enemies might call mischief.

All in all, the bishop can be given credit for singling out the best target for his opening salvo.

Mr. Robarts confirmed his intention of waiting upon the bishop, and was there at the appointed hour.

"Mr. Robarts," said the bishop, "I am very glad that you have been able to come to see me today. I know how busy you must be at Framley, especially at this time of year."

Now the hunting season had just started, and Mr. Robarts had at one time been known to follow the hounds rather more enthusiastically than is perhaps right in a man of the cloth. But he had no wish to commence hostilities as yet, so he merely informed the bishop that he was at his service.

The proposal the bishop then made surprised Mr. Robarts greatly. It was one which had its attractions for him, but which, on balance, he did not feel inclined to accept. He had, however, a counter proposal which he made to the bishop, and, after some discussion, Bishop Proudie agreed that the course proposed by the vicar of Framley should be followed.

Mr. Robarts rode home and wasted no time in telling his wife of the new development.

"Do you think you should tell him?" asked Mrs. Robarts.

"I did wonder,"said Mark. "But on reflection, I think no. Since I could not accept myself- and I am sure, my love, that you will agree with me that to accept would not be to our advantage, circumstanced as we are- since I could not accept myself, I thought it best to propose our friend. But the more I think of it, the more it seems to me that to give him notice will only be to give him time to think of reasons why he should also refuse. But once let him hear the proposal in the bishop's parlour, from the bishop's own mouth, and I think he will be hard put to decline. You remember how he has always been so particular about "obeying the bishop in all lawful matters within his authority". What could be more within the bishop's authority than this? And I am sure the appointment would please all our friends and confound our enemies."

The next morning therefore, it was Mr. Crawley, breakfasting serenely in his sumptuous rectory at Plumstead, who received a letter from the bishop inviting him to call at the palace.

Mrs. Crawley was convinced the letter boded ill. No good had ever come from the palace in the past.

But Mr. Crawley would not listen to her doubts.

"The bishop and I have had dealings in the past which in some respects were not what I should have wished them to be. But if he desires to consult me, he is certainly entitled to do so. I will wait to hear what he has to say before I consider further.

Having sent his reply, therefore, the following morning, after perusing a letter which had arrived that same day and which caused him much thought, Mr. Crawley drove into Barchester.

That one word "drove" brings out all the contrast between this journey and the last time Mr. Crawley had travelled to Barchester at the behest of Bishop Proudie.

Then he had walked, all the long weary miles from Hogglestock, in worn out boots and threadbare coat, with never a copper in his pocket nor a morsel to eat.

Now he travelled in a smart gig, which somehow seemed to come with Plumstead Rectory, with smart shoes and good broadcloth on his back, and the comfortable feeling of silver and even gold in his purse.

Then he had felt that all men's hands were against him, that all he met scorned and mocked him.

Now he was greeted politely by all who could in any way claim acquaintance, and saluted humbly by the servant to whom he gave his horse.

Then he had been kept waiting long hours before being permitted to stand before the bishop. Now he was ushered directly in, pressed to a comfortable armchair.

Then he had been treated as almost a criminal. Now he was offered the bishop's own hand.

Surely, the state of things had changed very much for Mr. Crawley.

How much they had changed was evident in the bishop's greeting.

"Mr. Crawley, " he said, "how good of you to come so promptly. I trust I see you well, and that Mrs. Crawley and all your family are in health?"

"I thank you, my lord, we are all blessed with excellent constitutions."

"I am glad to hear it. Glad indeed. Will you take a little Madeira?"

In these and further civilities such as Mr. Crawley had never before received at those hands the next few minutes were involved.

"Mr. Crawley," said the bishop at length, "I am particularly glad to see you today because the last time you were in this room we did not perhaps see eye to eye on a certain matter. I hope now to set things right between us, and to ensure that in future we shall be in accord."

Now the last time that Mr. Crawley had been in those apartments had been the occasion, he still consoled himself, of a famous victory over the bishop, or rather over the bishop's wife.

Mr. Crawley therefore replied only, "I trust, my lord, that I have never been in opposition to the lawful views of my bishop, and that I never shall be."

"Just so, just so. And therefore I have the greater pleasure in saying what I now wish to say. You will be aware, Mr. Crawley of the great loss there has been to the diocese since the departure of Dr. Grantly for higher things, and how sorely we feel his absence. The position of Archdeacon is now vacant. I have consulted on this point with Mr. Arabin, the Dean of Barchester, with Dr. Tempest, the Rural Dean, and with certain other clergymen of standing in the diocese, including your friend Mr. Robarts. They all agree with me that I could not do better than to offer the post to you. I do not think that a worthier, more learned and more pious man could be found in the whole see of Barchester, and I hope very much that you will consent to accept the preferment."

Mr. Crawley had once harboured very sore thoughts against his friend the dean on the subject of preferment. The sudden announcement of what would make his fortune both professionally and financially rendered him for the moment speechless.

"Come, come, Mr. Crawley, do say that you will accept. All your friends would urge you to accept. And it is so, well, so apt, don't you think. Dr.Grantly has been with us so long that it seems unnatural to think of the Archdeacon of Barchester and the Rector of Plumstead other than as one and the same. I need hardly add anything about the rewards on earth, but you must know that the position will double your income, and I am sure Mrs. Crawley would not be averse to that."

Mr. Crawley had by now had time to collect his thoughts, which indeed, had been till now largely on another subject.

"I have said, my lord, that I hope never to differ from you on any subject within your power. It is certainly within your power to recommend the new archdeacon, although I believe the choice will have to be approved by the archbishop. If you should see fit to recommend me, I can only thank you humbly for this mark of your confidence and trust that I shall perform the duties satisfactorily. What those duties are, I must confess, I have no very clear idea."

"Oh, your esteemed father in law will soon set you right on that. And there are plenty of others who will let you know if you go wrong. But I am sure that you will not go wrong. That is settled, then. Now may I tempt you to some Madeira?"

"One thing more, my lord, concerning the living of St. Ewolds."

"Yes, what of it. There will be no need for you to give it up, you know. You will well be able to afford a curate."

"I had thought of a curate, yes, my lord, but what you have just so kindly said has prompted me to another thought. Do I understand correctly that the presentation to the living of St. Ewolds is in the gift of the Archdeacon of Barchester? I believe that is how it came to me."

"Just so, Mr. Crawley, just so."

"Then I would be obliged if your lordship would allow me, after my institution, of course, to present to you an idoneous person for the living."

"Of course, of course, if he is really idoneous there can be no difficulty. I gather you have someone in mind."

"I have, my lord, but I will not name him until I have discussed the position with the person involved. I thank you for your kindness."

The interview lasted some few minutes more in the necessary civilities before Mr. Crawley was able to return in triumph to Plumstead. His reception there may well be imagined. The raptures of Mrs. Crawley, who but five years gone had been struggling to maintain her family on an income of £150 a year when she learned that her husband was soon to be in receipt of twenty times that sum are best not described.

Not that they were precisely selfish raptures.

"Just think of the difference it will make for our Jane," she said.

"I have no doubt that it may induce some young man who values money more than good sense and education to pay court to her. Whether or not that is a good thing, I leave to her to decide. But I know someone else to whom it should make a great difference indeed.

And he sat down to pen a reply to the letter he had received that morning.

"*Mr. Charles Crawley,*" he wrote, "*Lazarus College, Oxford.*"

"*My dear son,*

"*Your mother and I are both delighted to hear of the engagement you have contracted with your cousin Miss Amelia Toogood. The service which Mr. Toogood performed for me some years ago can never be adequately recompensed, and any further connection with his family can only be a good thing. The young lady herself is, to the best of my knowledge, thoroughly unobjectionable, and we will be delighted to welcome her at Plumstead as our daughter.*

"*I applaud your good sense in saying that the wedding cannot be for some time yet, as you have a living to find and no means to support a wife. I know that Mr. Toogood has a great many daughters and limited means to provide dowries. However, I think that I may be able to find a way round the difficulty. By the end of the term you will have taken orders. When you had done so, it was my intention to offer you the curacy of my old parish of St. Ewolds. The stipend is £150 a year. I know, none better, how difficult it is to bring up a family as gentlefolk on such an amount, and could only offer this as something faute de mieux. However, today I have had good news from an unexpected source, the bishop himself. I am to be Archdeacon in place of Dr. Grantly. The living of St. Ewolds is in the gift of the archdeacon, so that I can now promise you that in the event of your marriage, you shall* be, not curate, but vicar of St. Ewolds, with the full income of £350 a year on which your family have subsisted most adequately these five years past. With this assurance, I hope you will lose no time in naming the day on which all who love you will be made happy.

"Your mother and sister send their best sentiments, and I remain,

"Your loving father,
Josiah Crawley."

As Mr. Crawley set down his pen he could be forgiven for feeling that the Lord had indeed comforted him after his afflictions.

Chapter Eleven

THE BISHOP'S NEIGHBOURS

The neighbours to whom Bishop Grantly referred were that most trite of all ménages, a newly married couple, but lately returned from their honeymoon. This alone would have given them reason enough to go out into the world, to give dinners and parties and attend those given by others. But apart from this, they were much in demand, both as hosts and guests, by that part of London which goes by the name of "society" for reasons much more compelling.

The reader will no doubt be already familiar with the name and character of Mr. Plantagenet Palliser. Those conversant with the corridors of Westminster will have met him in committee rooms and in the house, while devotees of Barsetshire will remember his frequent visits to Courcy Castle. It was these visits, coinciding with those of one Lady Dumbello, which had given rise to a certain scurrilous rumour concerning Mr. Palliser and the lady. There had been no truth in the rumour, no truth at all, although many had taken it seriously including one on whom Mr. Palliser greatly depended. Mr. Palliser had decided because of this that perhaps there ought to be some truth in it, but the lady's thoughts had not coincided with his, and the matter had been resolved in a way perfectly satisfactory to her and her family, although not perhaps so satisfactory to Mr. Palliser.

Now Lady Dumbello, before her marriage to the eldest son of a marquis, had been Griselda Grantly, and the bishop's eldest daughter. She had ceased, of course, to be a Grantly on her marriage, and had almost ceased to be a daughter - in her own eyes at least, although not in those of her father.

Doctor Grantly had taken the rumours very seriously. He had been only too glad to be convinced of their falsehood, and had been more than ever conscious of the tact and good sense of his daughter, qualities which she had obviously inherited from her father.

Doctor Grantly had taken his daughter's innocence in respect to these rumours as also establishing the innocence of the gentleman involved. He had therefore come to have a feeling towards Mr. Palliser as of one unjustly slandered by the world, and this had made him well-disposed to the gentleman before ever he had met him. The meeting itself was almost inevitable once the bishop had begun to frequent the corridors and drawing rooms of Westminster, and when it took place neither side was disappointed. Each found in the other a gentleman of perfect good breeding and deportment, ready to be agreeable to those who were agreeable in return, with tastes and likings that complemented each other.

Neither Mr. Palliser's politics nor Doctor

Grantly's religion proved any obstacle to their growing regard for each other. It has to be said, nevertheless, that it would have taken quite strong efforts on Mr. Palliser's part to deter Doctor Grantly. For, apart from the predisposition already mentioned, there was another factor which greatly moved the bishop. Stout champion of his rights and prince of the church though he was, he was also – I fear no other word will do – something of a snob. He felt himself constrained to view his own daughter as scarcely mortal once she had married and become entitled to call herself a countess now and a marchioness hereafter. Honours such as this he could not help feeling partook in some small way of the divine.

Now Mr. Palliser had married Lady Glencora McClusky, the only child of the old Lord of the Isles, whose title and rank were almost regal in their honour and antiquity. Moreover, Mr. Palliser was himself ere long to be a duke.

To say, or even imply, that Doctor Grantly toadied to Mr. Palliser would be to do him a grave injustice. Nevertheless, there was something in his bearing which showed that he knew that he had to do with no ordinary mortal. Mr. Palliser himself unconsciously appreciated this, and, while the most democratic of men in principle, was much more comfortable so. The acquaintance had consequently developed into real friendship.

That the habit had developed of the Pallisers calling on the Grantlys owed more, however, to Lady Glencora. Mr. Palliser, while perfectly amenable to all his social obligations, was not a demonstrative man, and quite capable of believing that the few occasional words which sufficed for himself were all that other men sought from an acquaintance.

Not so, Lady Glencora. For her, friends were to be cultivated always, to visit and to entertain, to share gossip, thoughts, opinions and, above all, time. To know that a friend of hers was within reach and not spend at least part of the day together was, to her, inconceivable. She was young as yet, and had not learnt to count and define her friends carefully, with the result that those friends were many and her time very much taken up. Whether she will ever learn to be more careful in her selection of those she calls her friends is a story which only time will tell. But the Bishop she had certainly included in that circle which was much wider than her husband's. He was "an old dear" and "such fun" and "not at all the stuffy clergyman" and she was as determined that he should one day be archbishop as that her husband should one day be prime minister.

She was equally delighted to meet the guests of her favourite, and insisted that they attend her ball the following evening.

"Do come," she entreated. "It will be full of duty bores, whom Plantagenet cannot help having. We are in sore need of the other sort. And I am sure Miss Dale would not miss the opportunity to stand up in a London ball. It is quite unfair of you married ladies to begrudge her the chance."

As none of the married ladies in the room had ever thought of such a thing, this was rather unfair of Lady Glencora. But she was used to carrying her ideas through, and on this occasion, as on most, she prevailed, and the ladies of the house were left to consider what they had to wear which would not disgrace the most fashionable house in London.

Chapter Twelve

LADY GLENCORA'S PARTY

The gas street lamps of Park Lane shone down on the puddles from the afternoon's rainstorm, their yellow glow reflecting like ghostly flowers. They also shone on the coaches of the throng of visitors to the house of Mr. Plantagenet and Lady Glencora Palliser. Lady Glencora's parties had established a reputation for themselves such that anyone in London with any aspirations to being in the best society considered them to be one of the crowning events of the season. An invitation in itself was a mark of success – a guarantee that one had arrived - and many were the dowagers of Mayfair and Belgravia who laboured industriously to acquire one. All Lady Glencora's balls were sought after, but this occasion in particular had been especially coveted by the haut monde, as it was rumoured that not only the Prime Minister, but even royalty would be in attendance. The swarms on this night were therefore particularly thick.

None of this was known to any of the ladies of the Grantly party, although the Bishop was well aware of how things stood, and Major Grantly had some notion. They were quite unprepared for the crowds and the commotion. The brightness and heat of the large reception room left them blinking for a moment. After the servants had taken their things, there was none of the formal lining up to greet and be greeted by the host and hostess which had perhaps been expected. They were merely announced and left to make their own way.

The Bishop was almost immediately accosted by a fellow clergyman and dragged into the card room to make a fourth at whist. The Major also found professional acquaintances to converse with. Old Mrs. Grantly was then whisked away by another lady of similar clerical caste to listen to a newly returned missionary in another room. Lily and Grace, however, knew no-one within sight, and were left standing rather awkwardly at the side of the room.

"Well," said Lily, "aren't we the country bumpkins."

"Is there nobody here you know from the last time you were in London?" asked Grace.

"Mrs. Thorne and Bernard both lived very quietly, I suppose. I never was at anything like this before. We shall just have to compose ourselves to being wallflowers."

They had not been there long, however, before Lady Glencora spied their discomfiture and came hastening to the rescue.

"Let me introduce a young man without whom Plantagenet would have ever so much more trouble with his decimal currency than he does." Whereupon she half turned and tugged at the sleeve of a gentleman who had been speaking quietly to Mr. Palliser for the past few minutes, and whose back had been turned to Lily and Grace ever since they entered the room.

"Mr. Eames, Mrs. Grantly, Miss Dale. Mr. Eames, I am sure you would not refuse to be a guardian and protector for the evening to a beautiful young lady like Miss Dale."

The young man addressed seemed to start, but that may only have been the effect of being so suddenly drawn from one conversation to another.

He bowed in as accomplished a manner as any courtier.

"Thank you, Lady Glencora, for proposing such a delightful task. Any gentleman would be more than willing to oblige you with such advantage to himself. But, in any case, Miss Dale and I are old friends. And Mrs. Grantly is my cousin."

"Well!" said Lady Glencora. "What a little family party! But why did you not tell me? I see there is some mystery here. I must warn you that I cannot abide mysteries and I will have no peace until I have found it out. You must tell me all there is to tell."

But her attention at this moment was diverted by the harsh nasal bray of a gentleman in her husband's party a few feet away.

"Oh dear!" she said, "I see old Huffle Scuffle has cornered poor Plantagenet and I must fly to the rescue. Mr. Eames, do help me with one of your set-downs. You know you are the only person old Huffle is afraid of. Please excuse us Mrs. Grantly, Miss Dale, but do not go away, I beg you. We shall both return."

This left the ladies again unattended, but had the advantage that it gave Grace and Lily leisure to discuss the turn of events.

"Well!" said Grace. "Imagine little Cousin Johnny in such company, and so valued by them. But you are very quiet, Lily. Were not you surprised to meet him? How many years is it now?"

"Five years six months and two days," replied Lily abstractedly, "I have always said that nothing about Johnny Eames would ever surprise me. I hardly knew him with his beard and dressed so finely. And his manner, quite the swell. But I did not expect to meet him."

Now between Miss Dale and Mr. Eames certain things had passed in days gone by. All the party present knew of those things, and all had their own thoughts on how they should have ended. But it was not a subject which any of them cared to raise at that juncture .

"Well!" said Grace. "I hardly know where to start. To meet someone with whom one has been so intimately connected in the past, and after so many years. And in such company. But we will speak of something else if it gives you pain my love."

"It will never give me pain to speak of Johnny Eames, Grace. I should have thought you would know that. Just because we have fallen out of the habits we had when we lived in Allington and he in Guestwick does not mean that we cannot still be the best of friends."

"Oh, Lily! As if that was what I meant! But you always did affect to undervalue your own emotions."

"Oh, emotions! Those are articles a poor old maid like me cannot afford. But why you should think I should be afraid to meet a dear old friend of the family I cannot say."

Grace was meditating a rejoinder to the effect that she found such a reply less than ingenuous, but her meditations were interrupted by the return of the gentleman himself.

"I was sorry to have to leave you so soon," he said, "but I fear that Lady Glencora's commands are always obeyed in this house."

"Yes," replied Lily, "I think that Lady Glencora is rather used to getting her own way. But who was that very loud gentleman she wished you to speak to?"

Johnny laughed.

"He is rather loud, isn't he? That was Sir Raffle Buffle, the Chairman of the Board of Inland Revenue. Mr. Palliser is obliged to come much into his company just at the moment with this decimal currency project of his. And I, of course, can hardly avoid it, since I am Permanent Secretary of the Board."

"Permanent Secretary!" exclaimed Grace. "Isn't that rather grand?"

Johnny laughed again.

"Well, it keeps me in comfort. But these government boards are all the same, most of the members are only there for the look of it and all the work is done by one or two only."

"Meaning the secretary, I suppose," said Lily.

"The secretary of course, but others sometimes. Usually it's either the secretary or the chairman who run things, and often it's a fight between the two of them as to who has the mastery."

"Lady Glencora obviously thinks that in this case it is the secretary."

"That's a matter of opinion, of course, but I never stood any nonsense from Sir Raffle in the old days when I was his private secretary, and I think I've had the measure of him ever since. But why are we wasting time talking about him? Tell me all about Allington. I was so sorry to hear that you had left the Small House."

"Well, there is someone else living there now, you know."

"Not at this minute there isn't. I saw old Mr. Kornhopper on the Strand only this morning. Is your cousin in town too? I haven't seen him since his marriage. What a jolly girl Arabella Kornhopper was, but whatever you do, don't get Lady Glencora on to the subject of the father. She can go on about "Old KKK", as she calls him, for hours. But here I am prosing on without letting you speak. Do tell me all the latest news from Allington and Guestwick, and even Barchester if you have nothing better."

Whatever Lily might have had to say on the subject, however, was cut short by the striking up of the music in the adjoining ballroom, which rendered it obligatory for Mr. Eames to enquire if Miss Dale were engaged for the dance. Very soon, then, they were waltzing in the midst of the glittering throng of the very highest society of the capital.

This new Johnny, so confident, so polished, so

unhobbledehoyish, Lily found rather disconcerting, and instead of continuing their conversation, she was reduced to complimenting him on his dancing.

"Well, you see, I've had some practice since the last time I danced with you. And, of course, the footing is easier."

Seeing her blank look, he continued,

"Surely you remember the lawn at the Small House. That carefully arranged impromptu dance under the moonlight. How young we all were then, you and Bernard and Bell and Doctor Crofts and...."

He stopped short.

"Well, we were all young once," he concluded lamely.

"I know what was in your mind," said Lily. "You can utter the name of Adolphus Crosby in my presence. The fever is long since spent."

"Is it? Is it? Well, that is the way with youthful fevers, I dare say. Tell me, have you been riding in the park yet?"

And with such commonplaces the remainder of the dance passed. On returning Lily to her seat it was absolutely necessary that Grace should be asked for the next dance, and thereafter there were other young ladies to be attended to. As the evening progressed, Lily could not help noticing that one young lady in particular seemed to be singled out. Mr. Eames happened to be dancing with her when the Bishop emerged from the card room, and Lily took the opportunity to make enquiry of him.

"Oh, that's the Honourable Claudia Palliser, a distant cousin of our Mr. Palliser. She and young

Eames have been seen out together rather a lot lately."

"She appears to be rather an elderly young lady," said Lily.

"As to that, I would not venture to comment. She seems a pleasant enough girl to me, and reasonably intelligent for her sex. There are so many Pallisers about that one forgets just what relation she is to the Duke. But they all stick together and, of course, none of them is exactly penniless. He could do a lot worse for himself."

Lily made no further comment. To say that she refused all further invitations to the floor would be an untruth, but she found that she recollected none of them. Only three further events in the evening impressed themselves upon her.

The first of these was the return, as promised, of Lady Glencora.

"You must forgive me." She said. "But, you know, a hostess at one of these affairs is not her own mistress. Now, do tell me all about your youth in the country with Mr. Eames. I dare say you were childhood sweethearts. He seems so much a necessity here in London that one forgets he must have had a life of his own before he became so metropolitan. He is so clever that he has even impressed Plantagenet, and he quite frightens me sometimes with the things he knows about. And there are times when he seems so very preoccupied, almost sad. I am sure he must have a secret. Perhaps you can tell me what it is."

Lily's reply to this was, disappointing though it may be to relate, not as satisfactory to Lady

Glencora as the latter had hoped and did nothing to shake Lady Glencora's conviction that there was a "mystery" afoot. The minister's wife therefore resolved to find all about it by other means, and to devote the resources at her disposal to its unravelling and its satisfactory conclusion. What that satisfactory conclusion might be remains to be seen, but the resources at Lady Glencora's disposal were indeed formidable.

The second diversion occurred at the buffet, where Lily found herself next to Miss Claudia Palliser.

"Oh yes," Miss Palliser was saying to her companion, " Only a little further trouble will secure him. Of course he is only a plain Mister – unless you believe that tale about his relation to the old Earl – but he is a man who is going to make his way. My cousin thinks very highly of him. And he is well off. Everyone knows that. No, he will do very nicely."

This was said in a loud voice which Lily could not help finding affected, and, although no names were mentioned, she found herself strangely discommoded by what she had heard.

The other event occurred just as the Grantly party was leaving. The Bishop, and the Major being both occupied with their respective spouses, Lily found herself unattended on the doorstep, until an arm was offered to help her into the carriage.

"Here is my card," said Johnny. "Do come to tea on Friday."

Chapter Thirteen

THE DELIGHTS OF THE CAPITAL

The morning after the ball was inevitably accompanied by feelings of heaviness and anti-climax. The gentlemen of the party being occupied with the concerns which had brought them to the metropolis, were up and about their business long before the ladies had leisure to wish for amusement, and were consequently of little help in dispelling these emotions. Mrs. Susan Grantly, in any case, was not an early riser, and rarely appeared before the sun was at its height.

Lily and Grace had just finished breakfast and were settling down to talk over the previous evening when the doorbell rang and the maidservant entered to announce

"A gentleman to see Miss Dale, mum."

Lily and Grace looked at each other with perhaps one thought.

"Did he not give his name ?" asked Grace.

"No, mum, but he said he was an old friend."

"I know no-one in London," said Grace, "I can only think of one person it could be. Do you wish to see him, Lily, or shall we not be at home?"

"I am always willing to see an old friend. Please show him in."

The speculations which had certainly occurred to Grace were then put to an ignominious rest by the entrance of a rather stout young gentleman whom she had certainly never met before.

"Oh, Siph," exclaimed Lily, "what a surprise. I didn't even know you were in London. But let me introduce you to my dear friend. Mrs Grantly, may I present to you Mr. Onesiphorus Dunn, an old friend of Mrs. Thorne's, and my cavalier last time I stayed in London?"

"Not so old but what you can call me Siph." replied the gentleman. "I was wondering when you would get round to it. You never did before, you know, and all my friends do. I take that as a sign, so I do. And it's mighty pleased I am to meet you, Mrs. Grantly, at last. Hasn't the dear old bishop been singing your praises these months now, how you can talk Latin to beat the pope and write Greek like nobody since Thucydides? All that and yet no bluestocking is a great thing to meet with."

"You must take no notice of the way Siph rattles on, Grace," said Lily. "He is probably the most useful and agreeable person in London, and certainly the most harmless. He was very kind to me on my last visit."

Grace hardly knew what to make of such relaxed manners, but decided that there could be no harm in following Lily's example and that a reply in kind might at least have the effect of moderating their visitor's exuberance.

"Your parents must have been tolerable Grecians themselves, Mr. Dunn, to have burdened you with such a Christian name, if I may be allowed both the pun and the familiarity."

"Oh, and a burden it is, which I have to bear my whole life. But then, bearing burdens is my lot, in life as in name. Today, for instance, I am charged with the task of shopping in Bond Street for a birthday gift for a young lady of my acquaintance, and it occurred to me that the burden would be much lighter if shared. Could I prevail on you two charming ladies to give me the great pleasure of your company for the morning?"

Lily and Grace exchanged glances which confirmed their accord.

"I should be delighted to take this opportunity of furthering our acquaintance, Mr. Dunn," said Grace. "And I am sure that Miss Dale is of the same mind."

A morning in the retail palaces of the metropolis was ideally calculated to dispel the flatness left by the previous nights exertions, and Mr. Dunn proved the perfect escort on such an exhibition. He was always there when wanted with a comment or suggestion, and never obtrusive when not wanted. He knew exactly where to go for whatever was asked for, how much to pay, and what directions to give for delivery.

Above all, he did not let his own errand intrude on the ladies' time. Indeed, it seemed that he had quite forgotten about it, and on Grace's recollecting that she had promised to call on her cousin Mr. Toogood that morning he insisted on calling a cab and accompanying them.

Mr. Toogood's office, while perfectly respectable, was not in the fashionable part of London, and it seemed that the cabman had very little idea himself of where to find it. He drove through the City and into a maze of narrow streets with dark courts opening of them. The cab was delayed at the mouth of one of these courts by a dray unloading beneath a sign proclaiming,

"Burton and Bangles, Himalaya Wines."

"Himalaya Wines, indeed." Snorted Siph. "I dare say they charge mountainous high prices for them."

He had barely finished congratulating himself on his wit, when there emerged from the court a person whose dress proclaimed him a gentleman, though his whereabouts and demeanour might not. His face was shrouded from the occupants of the cab by the brim of his hat. His garments, though well cut and of respectable material, were old and shabby. His shoes were scuffed and his linen was none of the cleanest, while his unsteady gait and the odour of the gin shop that hung about him proclaimed that, early as the day might be, he had already had recourse to liberal amounts of liquid refreshment. Finding the motions of the road beneath his feet not to his liking, he availed himself of the handle of the cab door to steady himself, and in doing so raised his eyes towards the occupants.

The face which he lifted up to the window of the cab was red and puffy, the nose a mass of broken veins. It had not known the attentions of a razor for some time. The sparse wisps of hair which escaped from beneath his hat were greying and lank. The eyes, likewise, were reddened and dull, but became sharper as they focussed on the passengers.

Lily could not quite suppress the gasp that came involuntarily to her lips, while Siph took one look and banged upon the driver's window, telling him to "Drive on, drive on."

The dray now moved off and the cab too, while Grace shot a look of bemused interrogation at Lily.

"Did you know that man?" she asked.

"That," said Lily, "was Adolphus Crosbie."

"Mr. Crosbie, I am afraid," said Siph, "has gone very much down in the world. His quarrels at the General Committee Office are the talk of the town, and they say that the Board are trying to have him dismissed. If they succeed his state will be even worse, for his debts are even more notorious. There are some who say it serves him right."

"Not I," said Lily. "But how could I ever have thought of him as Apollo!"

Chapter Fourteen

REFLECTIONS ON OLD ACQUAINTANCES

"How could I ever have thought of him as Apollo!"

So Lily had exclaimed on encountering the man to whom she had once been engaged to be married. He had appeared among the Dales at Allington, sponsored by Lily's cousin Bernard, like a creature from another world. A demigod he had arrived, and had quite attained pure divinity by offering for Lily. But, indeed, his world was not their world, as he had demonstrated, all too soon, when he had given Lily up for a creature only too mundane.

It is true that our ideas of the heavenly and the godlike are not an "ever-fixed mark". Lily had once thought of this man as Apollo. She had... not precisely thrown herself at his feet, but she had been prepared to believe that he was all that was best in this world, and that she could not do better than to follow his guidance in all things. It had not lasted long, but while it endured, it had been sweet.

She had made of him something very like an idol, and given him something closely akin to worship. Later, when the clay feet of her golden calf could no longer be denied, she had pretended to herself that they were also of her own making.

Even when the fever was over and she could see him in his true, shabby colours, she still told herself that though he might stoop to be untrue, she would not. "The Dales were ever constant."

But she could not help admitting to herself that her notions of an Apollo had changed somewhat over the years. Apollos of the type she had imagined in her youth were not to be met with nowadays. But there must be, somewhere, even in these degenerate times, a man with sufficient of the Apollonian about him to be worth knowing.

He should be wise, of course, and possess sufficient of beauty and of wealth. He should be highly thought of by his fellows, known as a man worth knowing. But above all, he should be dependable. He should be a strong fortress, a refuge in whom one could trust. It was a sad accident of fate that she should have given her heart to a man who had lacked the last quality, and should have turned sightless eyes upon one who had possessed it in abundance.

It was with mixed feelings therefore that Lily approached the call she had promised to make upon Johnny Eames. There had passed between them in years gone by such things as cannot lightly be forgotten. Twice they had very nearly been man and wife, and twice Lily had drawn back. Now, after a long interval, their paths had crossed again. And what a change there had been in both of them! The diffident, awkward, but painfully sincere youth had turned into a sophisticated gentleman, a worldly-wise man-about-town, whose heart was no longer on his sleeve, and whose thoughts and feelings - once so plain for all to see - were a mystery. Truly, Lily did not know what to make of the new Johnny.

So mixed, indeed, were her feelings that she thought it best to consult the Bishop as to the propriety of calling upon a single gentleman in his rooms in London. To one so used to following her own counsel, this was a departure indeed.

The Bishop looked at the card Lily had brought back from the ball.

"Nonsense, my dear," he said. "That is a flat in the Adelphi, one of the best addresses in London, for an unmarried gentleman, that is. Mr. Eames does very well for himself. You need feel no disquiet about calling there. And in any case, if you wish, Mrs. Grantly will go with you as chaperone. But, stay, Grace would be even better. She is just as much an old married lady, and she is the gentleman's cousin, is she not? What could be more proper?"

With such high ecclesiastical approval Lily could not put off the visit, and Friday afternoon saw the two young ladies alighting from the Bishop's carriage on the Strand.

Grace looked rather dubiously at the doorway with the uniformed porter.

"I just can't think of Cousin John living all by himself in a flat in 'one of the best addresses in London'. I'm sure it must be all bachelor squalor inside, with books and things all over the place, and lukewarm tea and a cake bought from a pastrycook, just like Charles's rooms at Oxford."

The rather formidable-looking porter informed

them that they were expected, and showed them up to the landing.

They were greeted at the door of the flat by Mr. Eames himself.

"Do come in," he said. "I've been looking forward to this ever since I saw you at the ball."

The parlour into which he showed them was not what they had been expecting. All was neat, clean and tidy. The furniture and floors shone with polish, the brass grate twinkled and the windows were spotless. The walls were adorned with pictures in the latest taste, which looked, to Lily's eye at least, to be original. The tea table was laid with an immaculate white damask cloth, set off by shining silver and delicate china. All in all, it was almost as far removed from 'bachelor squalor' as it was possible to be.

"Well," said Grace, "Bishop Grantly was right. You have done well for yourself, Cousin Johnny. But I never knew you had such taste. The carpets, the wallpaper, the curtains, the fittings! Forgive me, John, but I would never have thought you capable of creating such an effect."

"Oh, well, I suppose I didn't, you know. I believe I am not known for excellence in that line."

"I dare say you employed a decorator," said Lily.

"A decorator was employed, yes, but the choice of furnishings, papers, carpets, everything like that, I admit I left to the mistress of my household."

"The mistress of your household! John! You surely do not mean to tell us that you are married?"

"No, I am not married. I think I would have told you before now if I were. But my household does have a mistress, and she will be disappointed she missed your arrival. But she will be here directly, I am sure."

Both Grace Grantly and Lily Dale were properly brought up young ladies. The morals of one had been formed by a clergyman father, and of the other by a loving mother of the strictest principles. This announcement by their friend left them not knowing what to think. Could he possibly mean what he seemed to be saying?

The two ladies looked at each other in growing embarrassment.

"Surely not.," was the thought that had occurred to each, and each wondered who would be the first to ask the awkward question.

Their silence and consternation however were broken alike by the opening of the door and the entry of Mary Eames.

"Behold the mistress of my household," laughed Johnny. "What a sight your faces are! Surely you did not have anyone else in mind?"

Mary apologised for her errand, which had taken longer than planned.

"At the last minute Johnny must have Madeira Cake." she laughed. "I had to run across the street to get it. These desirable residences in London, you know, are so desirable that they lack such minor amenities as working kitchens."

There followed a period of general merriment over the object of Mary's quest, accompanied by cucumber sandwiches and Orange Pekoe. Much of the merriment concerned reminiscences of ancient history, of bygone days at the Small House, or in Guestwick. Lily, however, seeing at length how little a part in the conversation was played by Grace whose childhood had been spent far differently, and seeking a more general subject eventually hit on the expedient of admiring the works of art which adorned the walls and shelves.

"I was only ever in Italy the once," said Johnny, "and, as you know, I had no time then for doing the Grand Tour. Do, by the way, give my regards to Mrs. Arabin when next you see her. But I like to think I am not entirely uncultured, even if Old Masters are beyond me. I have one or two modern pieces which I think are not wholly without merit."

"I love the landscapes," said Lily. "But that canvas over the fireplace is rather gloomy, isn't it? A biblical subject, if I am not mistaken."

"Oh, Jael and Sisera. That was painted by a friend of mine, and has had rather a chequered history. The artist eventually married his model – a perfectly respectable young lady, by the way, comfortably off, too, not a professional artist's model – and the canvas was never sold. After a while, finding it brought back memories of events which neither Mr. nor Mrs. Dalrymple cared to recollect, they gave it to me. I am obliged to give it a prominent place, in case they call and find me neglecting their gift."

"Mr. Dalrymple?" asked Grace. "Conway Dalrymple? I have met him. He is a very fashionable artist, and mixes in society."

"All the paintings are beautiful," said Lily, " but I almost prefer these exquisite bronze figures. And the china is quite lovely."

"I know what you're thinking," said Johnny. "How can he possibly afford all this on his salary? Well, it is quite an abundant pittance, especially now that I am secretary to the Board, but, then, I have been very lucky. Lord de Guest of course was very generous to me in his will, which kept me in bread and butter and a moderate amount of jam in the old days, but then when Lady Julia died I was amazed. She had always lived so moderately that it should have been no great surprise to learn how much she had saved out of her jointure. But it was astonishing that she should leave it all to me."

"And who else should she leave it to?" asked Mary. "She had no relations except her Nova Scotia cousin whom she hated and who was bound to inherit the title and the estate. She had spent her life antagonising most of the county people around her. You were the only friend she had after her brother died, and you did save old Lord de Guest's life, under providence. I will never forget that day the note came about you and the bull. Mother didn't know whether to be more proud or upset."

This remark made it necessary to recount for Grace's benefit the tale of Lord de Guest and the bull, a tale which gave the ladies much occasion for exclamations of amazement and delight, while its hero flushed and muttered darkly into his teacup.

With such amusements the afternoon passed, and before they knew it it was time for the ladies to leave.

Grace was anxious for both Eameses to take tea at the Bishop's the following week.

"I am sure Mary will be delighted, thank you," said Johnny, "but I am very sorry to say that I will not be in town next week, or the week after. I leave tomorrow morning for Matchings, Mr. Palliser's house near Silverbridge. The decimals are being disagreeable again, and he cannot manage without me, or so he says. My own thought is that Lady Glencora needs someone to make up the numbers, but we shall see. But I will call the instant I return."

"Lady Glencora made no mention of a house party when she called at my father-in-law's yesterday." said Grace. "Not that there was any obligation on her to do so, of course. But the two families have become so intimate lately that I think she might have mentioned it."

"It is not so much a house party as a working party. Mr. Palliser needs to get all his details straight before he next reports to the House. There will only be those who can be useful .The duke will be there – the Duke of St. Bungay that is, for the Duke of Omnium never concerns himself with such matters – Mr. Grey and Mr. Finn. Mr. Bonteen has been prevailed upon to absent himself, thank goodness. As for the ladies, only wives, and Miss Claudia Palliser, to fetch and carry for Lady Glencora."

This news would have been subject for much exclamation and discussion, but further reflections were interrupted by the entry of the porter, with the news that "Mrs. Grantly's carriage was waiting".

The journey back to Mayfair was nowhere near long enough for adequate consideration of the new Johnny Eames. Still less did it afford time for Lily to convince herself that the inclusion of Miss Claudia Palliser in the Matchings party was very natural and only to be expected. And why on earth should she find cause for concern in the prospect of Miss Palliser and Mr. Eames shut up for a fortnight together in a country house?

Chapter Fifteen

MATCHING PRIORY

Everyone, of course, has heard of Matching Priory, the country seat of Mr. Plantagenet Palliser. Its charming scenery, its delightful atmosphere, its sumptuous comfort and picturesque setting are a byword among all who claim to belong to society. It is known to many more people than have ever set eyes upon it as 'the only place to stay in the country'.

At the time of which we are writing, however, its laurels were still largely to be won. Mr. Plantagenet Palliser had been given the house and estate by his uncle the duke upon his marriage to Lady Glencora McClusky, and still looked upon it as his place to retreat from the world. Those only were invited there who were either necessary or wanted. The great parties and receptions given by Lady Glencora to her husband's political allies, on which the fame of the house was to rest, were still things of the future. To be asked to Matching was a distinction, to be sure, but not to be asked was far from social death.

Johnny Eames, therefore, when he boarded the Silverbridge train at the Paddington station, did not particularly feel that he was one of the social and political elite of the capital. His feelings were rather those of resigned forbearance at two weeks of extra work at a time when he had a particular reason for not wishing to leave London. Matching, no doubt, would be very pleasant, and it was also very pleasant to know that he was considered almost indispensable by so many among the great and the good of the nation, but....

How many things are comprehended in that one word "but"! Of course he was flattered that the boy from Guestwick who had once been considered a rather dull companion for the ladies of the Small House at Allington should now be sought after by those who were in fact ruling the country. It was flattering, too, that they valued his advice so highly that it was felt to be essential for a great project which would change all their lives. He could make a long list of people – a list headed by his own chief, Sir Raffle Buffle – who would give much to be among the guests at Matching and to have the ear of Plantagenet Palliser. Great things were expected of Mr. Palliser, greater, that is, than merely becoming a duke in due course, and the numbers of those in the corridors of Westminster who simply itched for a chance to shine in his reflected light were legion. Any attention from that quarter was looked upon as a sure sign of good things to come in future.

But, all the same, there was no denying that this preferment – if preferment it was – had come at a most inconvenient time.

It had been some years now since he had severed

all connection with both Guestwick and Allington. The days he had spent there – the days of his youth and his young manhood - were in part the sweetest he had ever known. They were also the blackest. When his hopes had been dashed for the last time, as he stood on the bridge at Allington where once he had carved the intitials "LD", he had sworn to himself that he would have no further truck with such fancies, and would live his life without dreams. He had taught himself to do so, or thought he had, and the success of his teaching had been so great that men said of him that there was no more sensible and straightforward a person in London.

He had been living the life of a fashionable man about town, or at least he had been doing so while at the same time making a name for himself in his work . His days and his nights had been filled for him, and the time left for dreaming had become a burden he hardly felt any more. And now he had met Lily Dale again, after years of avoiding her, of avoiding all news of her, of any mention of her in his letters to and from his sister and his cousins. "Meine ruh ist hin," he did not quite say to himself. But somewhere, without articulating the words, he felt it, and as he sat in the carriage, waiting for the guard's whistle, he could not give to the subject of decimal currency quite the application for which he had made his name.

In this mood he bent over his papers, trying to force his mind to concentrate, and only dimly noticed the entry of another person into the carriage, and the eventual departure from the station.

They had been a few minutes on their way when a voice interrupted his thoughts.

"Mr. Eames, isn't it?"

Johnny looked up, and into the face of a gentleman seated opposite him. It was a face that looked, at first sight, stern and uncompromising, but was transformed with a smile when Johnny acknowledged his identity.

"Barrington Earle. We met at Mr. Palliser's the other day."

"How nice to see you again, Mr. Earle. Mr. Palliser often speaks of you."

"Not so often as he speaks of you, I dare say. 'Mr. Eames says this, Mr .Eames thinks that.' To listen to Mr. Palliser one would think that his great project could not conceivably succeed without you."

"Mr. Palliser is very kind. In fact all I do is try to find ways of making his suggestions work, especially in relation to the taxation system as it is, and, perhaps, as it ought to be."

"As it ought to be? Those are large words."

They fell into a conversation, in which it soon became clear that they agreed on many things. Mr. Earle was also going to Matching, and was obviously an old habitué. He had equally obviously known Mr. Palliser for many years. Johnny had a vague recollection that he held some important position in the Liberal party. Indeed, most of his comments and questions had a political slant to them and it soon appeared that they agreed on most things.

The conversation was congenial, and Johnny was agreeably surprised at the apparent esteem in which he was held by this associate of Mr. Palliser. This was as nothing, however, to the surprise with which he greeted the following remark.

"I wonder you have never thought of standing for parliament yourself, Mr. Eames. I am sure the Liberal Party would find you a safe seat, if Mr. Palliser can't lay his hands on a convenient borough."

"Are you serious, sir?"

"Deadly serious, I do assure you. In fact we need someone with local connections to fight the by-election at Barchester, and from what Mr. Palliser has been saying about you, and from what you have been saying to me, I think you would be just the man."

"Let me be clear about this, sir. Are you saying that if I chose to stand as a candidate I would be supported officially by the Liberal Party ?"

"I am, sir. And I am authorised to do so."

"Is this the way these things are normally settled? A casual conversation during a chance meeting in a railway carriage?"

"Hardly casual, or chance, I do assure you. I took this train deliberately to provide an opportunity of speaking to you. We have had our eyes on you for some time now."

"Well, I am flattered. But I must remind you sir, that I am one of Her Majesty's civil servants. If I were to stand for parliament I should have to give up my post. "

"Well, yes, and I know you would lose by it, financially. But everyone knows that you are not hard pressed for money, and that you only stay in your post for the pleasure of keeping down old Huffle Scuffle."

"That is certainly a gratification, I admit, but I am afraid that the rumours of my wealth are greatly exaggerated. And Members of Parliament are not remunerated in any way for their efforts."

"But think of the service you can do for your country. Think of the good you could do if you had the making of the nation's laws, rather than merely the administering of them. Think of the possibility of office."

"I will think of it. I do think of it. I am flattered, but you are asking me to give up a sure income, to give up a career which I have reason to believe is satisfactorily prospering in favour of a prospect of success which is at best aleatory. You must give me time to consider."

"Time? Well, yes, you have time. But the writs go out quite soon now. I need to know by the time we leave Matching or I will have to find someone else."

For Barrington Earle, while perfectly willing to be favourably impressed by Mr. Palliser's protégé, had a high notion of the honour he was conferring in making his request, and was not best pleased at the way it was received.

Johnny, however, perceived none of this from his companion's demeanour, and, what with further conversation and consideration of this novel suggestion the journey to Silverbridge passed more quickly than he had expected.

At their destination Mr. Palliser's carriage met

them so that there was none of the awkwardness of hiring conveyances which is so often to be met with at country stations. They were greeted on arrival at the house by Lady Glencora herself, who informed them that Mr. Palliser was engaged, and would meet them at dinner. He did not propose to call on their services that day in any case.

Dinner that night was as solemn an affair as Johnny could remember witnessing. Matching Priory had, of course, been but one of the smaller residences of the Duke of Omnium before he had made it over to his nephew. Even so, its grandeur put both Allington and Guestwick severely in the shade, and Johnny felt himself being overawed in spite of all his efforts.

"It's just as well it isn't Gatherum Castle," he thought. "Then I would feel put in my place."

There was a shortage of ladies at the table, and Johnny found himself with Barrington Earle to his left and Claudia Palliser to his right.

The lady was particularly attentive, seeming almost to take charge of the new guest.

"This is your first time at Matching, Mr. Eames, is it not?" she asked. "You must favour us with your presence more often."

"I would be delighted to do so," said Johnny, "if Mr. Palliser or Lady Glencora are good enough to ask me again."

"Oh, but Mr. Palliser thinks very highly of you, you know. He relies very heavily upon your work. In fact, he cannot do without you."

"I am sure Mr. Palliser can do very well without me. In the jungle of Westminster, he is the lion, and I am only the jackal who goes about after him to deal with the unconsidered trifles. And it may not suit Lady Glencora to have too much of his time at home taken up this way."

"Mr. Palliser will make his own mind up on that score, I do assure you. And in any case, if jackal you are, you are so much an improvement on the jackals Mr. Palliser has had of late – I am thinking particularly of Mr. Bott and Mr. Bonteen – that Lady Glencora quite dotes upon you by comparison."

"I am grateful for your confidence, Miss Palliser, although I wonder a little at the wisdom of naming such names. But perhaps the improvement, if any there be, is because they were political jackals and I am a civil jackal."

"Ah, there you have it. Civil is exactly what they were not, in the end. And I am sure that you are civil in every sense, Mr. Eames."

All this was very gratifying, but not nearly so much as the conversation when the ladies left the room.

"Well, Eames," said Mr. Palliser, "Earle tells me that you are about to join us in the house."

"Mr. Earle was kind enough to suggest it to me, and the idea is very tempting. But there are two things that give me to pause. The first is the rather sordid question of money. I should lose my place, you know, and the emolument is not to be lightly thrown away. And it is not just the money, either. I have worked hard to be where I am, and it is not impossible that I may go further. Sir Raffle himself once held the post I now occupy. Yet if I were sure that I could do more good in the house than in the department I would hesitate the less. But I find it hard to convince myself that I could be worthy of such an honour."

"My dear sir," put in Earle, " you have a very high notion of members of parliament. I do assure you there are as many rascals among them as in any other walk of life - rather more in fact."

"Mr. Earle exaggerates, perhaps, a little," said Mr. Palliser, "but in all seriousness, I should not have thought that you would let the question of money stand in the way of serving your country. Everyone knows that it is not your salary that keeps you in your work now, and that you could live perfectly well without it if you chose. I do not wish to be impertinent, but I have always understood that you have an income quite independent of your office, which enables you to act in the way you have done so often on points of principle. And as for the second point, let me say that I can think of no-one I would rather have on my side in the house."

"You are very kind, sir. I have promised Mr. Earle my answer before we leave this house, and I assure you I will think seriously on all you have said."

"That is all anyone can ask of you, Mr. Eames. And now, how do you think the income tax legislation should be framed to embrace quints and semi-tenths?"

The rest of the fortnight passed quickly enough - quicker, indeed, than anyone would have expected who did not know the personalities involved. The mornings were spent in solid work, but Mr. Palliser was not a hard taskmaster, and knew that the chances of his achieving anything lasting depended entirely on the goodwill of his assistants. He therefore made sure that he preserved that goodwill by the reasonableness of his demands. The afternoons were free for whatever his guests wished to do by way of business or recreation, while the evenings were for sociability with the ladies.

Here Johnny found himself the odd man out. All the other guests were married except for Barrington Earle, who was known as a confirmed bachelor. He was therefore thrown much in the company of Miss Claudia Palliser, the only unattached lady, and before the first week was out it had become a joke among the party that the pair were inseparable.

"When are we to wish you joy?" asked Lady Glencora on the Saturday evening.

Now Lady Glencora was known to be possessed of a sense of humour, but she was also known to have one of the keenest pair of eyes in London, and the question made certain of the other guests sit up.

Johnny passed it off with a comment as to the impossibility of thinking of such things on the eve of the Sabbath, which did well enough for the company but might be thought less than ingenuous in one who was no more than indifferent devout.

Miss Palliser, however, did nothing to contradict her cousin's assumption, and seemed to cling closer than ever that evening.

During the second week, Miss Palliser's attentions were even more marked, the more so as they might be thought to have had more opportunity of camouflage. The source of the camouflage was the arrival of more guests, whose effect was to dilute the political nature of the gathering.

The new arrivals were none other than Mr. Otis P. Kornhopper and his daughter. Lady Glencora had invited the ketchup magnate in a spirit of –it would be wrong to say mischief, so perhaps we had better say of - pure research, to see what effect the added ingredients would have upon the party. She looked forward to witnessing his effect on her husband and on certain of the more stuffy members of his set. In the face of Mr. Kornhopper's earnest entreaties, she had extended the invitation to include his daughter and her husband. Mr. Dale, however, being of the contrary political party, had felt that it would not do to be seen at the house of so prominent an opponent and had declined. Not so his wife, who was "Just dying to mix with all those dooks and earls" and could not see why there should be any objection.

Their presence certainly enlivened the party, especially as Mrs. Dale was effectively an extra young lady, albeit a young married lady. Indeed, her marriage was so recent that it was absolutely necessary to pay her certain attentions.

Miss Kornhopper – that is to say, Mrs. Dale- was a married lady, certainly. But she was also an American young lady, and used to exacting her due of tribute from the males around her. Mr. Palliser and the duke, and indeed most of their set were beyond the reach of her snares, rendered immune by age and length of matrimony. Not that the disparity of age, in strict chronology, that is, was always so great. But Mr. Palliser, for instance, had, in Lady Glencora's words "been born a greybeard".

The only legitimate targets for her wiles were consequently Johnny and Barington, and the latter had long since armoured himself against all female weapons.

Her broadsides, therefore were concentrated on Johnny, as the only unattached young man in the house, and it was a delight to see the manoeuvres of both Claudia and Arabella in their competition for his services.

To say that Mr. Eames gave the young ladies no encouragement might not perhaps be strictly correct, if ease of manner and general complacency can be construed as encouragement. Anything more than that, however, depended entirely upon the eye of the beholder.

Lady Glencora asked her relation outright on the Tuesday evening, after the ladies had left the gentlemen to their port.

"Tell me straight, Claudia, is there anything between you and Mr. Eames?"

"Why do you ask that, Lady Glencora?"

"I ask because you have hung on his arm all this last week, you have followed him about like a lost dog, you have laughed at all his jokes, exclaimed at all his remarks and had barely a word for anyone else. Are you in love with him?"

"Lady Glencora, may I speak frankly to you?"

"I wish you would, although when someone asks

that question it usually means they are getting ready to lie to you."

"I will try not to lie to you. You know how I am placed. I was brought up on the fringes of a wealthy family, on the edge, as it were of luxury, used to all the comforts of life, but without any provision for obtaining them other than my name and looks. My father died as near penniless as it is possible for a Palliser to be. My mother was nobody in particular and her money went too. I have no money, no property, no special skills or abilities. I am thirty years old and I do not want to spend the rest of my life as a companion to some wealthy lady, even to one as indulgent as yourself. The gentlemen I usually meet are either spoken for or have blatantly commercial motives. I have been looking at Mr. Eames, and I find that he will do."

"Has he given you any cause for hope? Has he spoken?"

"No, but I think that before the next week is out he will do so."

"Mr. Eames has a history, you know. There is a broken heart in there somewhere."

"I know nothing of broken hearts, but I would be a good wife to him. Tell me that you approve."

"It cannot be called a good match for a Palliser. If what they say about his connection with Earl de Guest is true it would not be the first time the bar sinister has appeared in our family, but even so. Otherwise he is nobody. A very pleasant, useful nobody, and a gentleman, but nobody to consider. But I believe he has money."

"They say he owns half the Great Western

Railway and has a share in many other interests. His salary is £1200 a year and I know he has dividends and interest besides."

"You are sounding like a tax man yourself. You still haven't answered me, you know. I must repeat myself. Do you love him?"

"I will repeat myself, too. He will do."

This was hardly satisfactory to Lady Glencora, but she resolved that Mr. Eames must take his chance.

Mr. Eames, meanwhile, was perfectly unaware of any feminine designs, and continued – when not waylaid by Mrs. Dale -to walk on the terrace with Miss Palliser, to fetch and carry for her, to pick up her dropped handkerchiefs and generally do all the things a lover may be supposed to do.

During the course of the week the general expectation grew, and on the Thursday evening, Miss Palliser had a little word with Lady Glencora, who in turn spoke to Mr. Palliser.

What she said to him surprised that gentleman.

"Are you sure, my dear?" he asked. "I cannot say that I have had any such notion."

"His attentions have been quite marked." said Lady Glencora. "You must be the only one in the house who has not noticed. Claudia tells me that he has made it quite plain from his manner to her that he considers her in the light of more than common friendship. I really think you should ask him what his intentions are."

"But has he truly asked her to marry him?"

"As to that, I could get no definite answer. I rather think not, or Claudia would have said so.

As to whether he has given her reason for expectations, I do not know."

"It's a confounded bore, but I dare say I had better do it."

The following morning, Johnny found himself summoned to Mr. Palliser's study.

"Mr. Eames," said Mr. Palliser, motioning to a chair ,"I find that I am called upon to ask you certain questions about your intentions with regard to my cousin Miss Claudia Palliser. I do not wish to be impertinent, but I have been given to believe that the attentions which you have been paying to her during your stay here have given rise to certain expectations. I must beg you for clarification."

"May I ask the nature of these expectations?" asked Johnny, still unclear of the purpose of the interview.

"In short, my cousin believes that you have matrimony in mind."

"I have to say that I am honoured by your cousin's good opinion, sir, but I assure you that such a subject was never in my mind for a moment. Miss Palliser has been a pleasant companion during my time here, and I have endeavoured to make the time equally pleasant for her. My attentions to Miss Palliser, and everything I have said to her, have been no more than courtesy required. I am sorry if they have given rise to expectations of greater things, but I really cannot see that I have given Miss Palliser greater cause for such opinions than I have given Lady Glencora or the duchess. I regret greatly that you have had this trouble, sir, and should be very sorry to lose your good opinion, but you must admit the proposal to be impossible when I tell you that my heart has long been engaged elsewhere."

"People do marry when their hearts are engaged elsewhere."

Mr. Palliser was perhaps thinking of certain episodes in his own past when he made this answer.

"And often such marriages do not turn out badly. But I suggest Mr. Eames that you perhaps be more on your guard in future. I do not think the young lady's heart will be broken in this case, but who can tell? It would be a pity to get a reputation as a breaker of hearts."

It may perhaps be thought that Mr. Palliser had let Mr. Eames off lightly. But he was no fool, and this was not the first time he had been called upon to undertake such an interview on behalf of the young lady. In his opinion, she was all too prone – desperate was a word he did not care to use in connection with young ladies – to seize at anything which might be considered an overture to marriage, provided, that is, the gentleman in question was "comfortably off". He told nothing but the truth when he said that he did not think there would be any hearts broken.

That is not to say that there was no embarrassment, or even discomfort. Mr. Palliser did not find himself obliged to mention his talk with Mr. Eames to Miss Claudia, but he could not avoid discussing the subject with his wife.

"It's no go," Lady Glencora said to Claudia later that same evening. "Planty has had a word with

Mr. Eames, and he protests that 'his affections are engaged elsewhere', though no-one has ever known him so much as look at a woman for years. You will have to find someone else, my dear."

For the rest of his stay at Matching, Johnny found himself much occupied with business. This inevitably meant closer association with Mr. Palliser, but that was in any event preferable to the danger of coming within the sights of the lady, now that he knew himself to be her target.

The combination of eating and sleeping in decimals and doing his best not to "find the lady", afforded him very little time to consider the proposition Earle had made to him on their way down.

It was only in the railway carriage on the way back that the subject was raised again.

"I tell you what, Earle," Johnny said, "let me consult some friends and see how the land lies as to money. You don't really want an answer this minute, do you?"

"Oh, there's not that much of a hurry really. It would be such a bore finding someone else now. I have to go to the Chilterns' tomorrow, but I will be back in town at the end of the month. Let me know then, will you? Now can we have that confounded blind down? Shocking glare there is in these new carriages, and a terrible rattling and creaking they do make."

From all of which it may be gathered that Mr. Earle had celebrated perhaps too enthusiastically the night before.

Chapter Sixteen

NEWS FROM THE COUNTRY

Mr. Kornhopper and his daughter spent only one night at Allington before returning to London. From Allington they were accompanied by Mr. Bernard Dale, who was still quite enough in love with his wife to wish not be unnecessarily separated from her.

He also retained sufficient family feeling to ensure that a visit to his cousin was one of the first he made in town.

The arrival of the new Mrs. Dale in the Bishop's drawing room was calculated to raise ecclesiastical eyebrows.

"Well, I declare," drawled Arabella, as she sat down to the tea and biscuits provided. "So this is bishop Grantly's palace. If you hadn't told me I should have said it was a perfectly ordinary house, just like any other in the street."

"It is much like any other." replied the bishop, who chanced to be at home that morning and was never averse to taking his share in any hospitality offered by his household. "That's just the beauty of it. No great draughty halls, no miles of useless corridors, gas lighting, hot water, all modern conveniences – and no room for hangers-on. Dioceses generally run themselves, you know, if left to themselves, and here I can do just that, with no temptation to be forever meddling simply because there's a great warren of offices to fill up with underlings."

"But a palace ought to be grand. It ought to be imposing, majestic even. Where is your audience chamber, where is your throne room? I do so long to see your throne."

"My dear young lady, episcopal state is not royal, you know. A bishop's throne is kept in his cathedral, as mine will be, as soon as I get myself a cathedral. I assure you that in the meantime I do not feel the want of it."

"Of course not, my dear," put in the elder Mrs. Grantly. "We all know that you are quite capable of ex cathedra pronouncements without it."

Now Mr. and Mrs. Bishop had had a little disagreement that morning and were perhaps not in the finest state of Christian charity towards one another.

Bernard, meanwhile, had turned to Lily.

"How are Bell and my aunt?" he asked. "Have you heard from them since you left Barchester? We hear so little at Allington these days."

"Bell will be here soon, you know. I'm sure she will be very pleased to see you both. Mother writes that she is well, but feeling rather matronly, by which I take her to mean that she is no longer as young as she once was. But nothing ever happens at home, of course."

"Nothing ever happens! In Barchester! And to

think we once considered it the big, wicked city."

"I think it might have been wicked enough, as cathedral cities go, once upon a time. But I believe Mrs. Proudie did a thorough job of exorcising most of the wickedness, and Bishop Proudie keeps up the tradition now that she is gone. But what have you been doing?"

"Oh, the life of a country squire. Uncle Christopher would have been proud of the way I have borne with all the farmers of Allington, and most of the farmhands, too , who all seem to think that the squire is the only man who can deal with their problems. There has been no excitement there, either. But Arabella has been away, mixing with the high and mighty, at Matching Priory, no less. And, even more strange, she met an old friend of ours there. You will never guess, but I will get her to tell you all about it herself."

Lily thought that she could guess very well, but she was in a complaisant mood, and let her cousin have his little surprise. Her astonishment when Arabella proclaimed that she had met John Eames at Matching was a very civilised and convincing counterfeit – which was very soon converted into genuine amazement at the news which followed.

"I never met Mr. Eames before, of course," said Arabella, "but he seemed to me a very pleasant sort of gentleman. And I know you are all old, childhood friends, so I'm sure you will be glad to hear that he is about to make what I believe you call over here "a most advantageous connection" Yes, indeed he is."

"Whatever can that be?" asked Lily.

"Well, I know there has been no announcement or anything of that sort as yet, but I can tell you now that he is going to marry the niece of a duke. There, I knew that would make you stretch your eyes. Yes, believe you me, you'll soon enough read in the papers about the engagement of Mr. John Eames to the Honourable Claudia Palliser, niece to the Duke of Omnium. Now, what do you say to that?"

Lily found that she could say nothing, and there would have been an awkward break in the conversation if Grace, seeing her friend's discomfiture, had not stepped in.

"Mr. Eames is my cousin, you know, and all our family are particularly fond of him. We would be very glad to hear of anything which would make him happy. But, tell me, on what do you base this rather extraordinary news? I assure you that none of his family had any inkling of it."

"Neither did Mr. Eames himself, I think, before he went down to Matching. They had been there a week together when I arrived, and by then it was accepted by all the gathering as quite a matter of course. Why, you've never seen anything as like a pair of lovers as the two of them. Never apart, except when the gentlemen were at work, always considered a couple, sly winks and nods all round when they were mentioned. Mr. Palliser even took Mr. Eames aside one night for a talk that was definitely not about decimal coinage. What else could it be?"

What else, indeed? Lily's part in the remainder of the conversation was rather less than her usual share. She got through it, somehow, and found herself rather relieved when the visitors had departed.

"Well," said Grace, "what do you think of this news about Johnny?"

"I have always said," replied Lily, "that John Eames was fit to marry any lady in the land, and I am sure I wish that they will both be happy. And now, if you will excuse me, dear Grace, I have a headache and I think I will lie down."

The night that followed, however, in which her thoughts gave her no rest, proved less than an adequate cure for her headache, and breakfast time the following morning found Lily still incapable of participating fully in Grace's joy at her cousin's new-found happiness.

"Isn't it wonderful news about Johnny and Miss Palliser?" said Grace, barely giving Lily time to sit down. "I am so looking forward to seeing them both when they get back from Matching. I am sure that they will have lots to tell us. Just think, my cousin's cousin will be a duke."

For, intelligent and educated as she was, Grace was not entirely above a little snobbishness of the old-fashioned, non-intellectual kind, and the prospect had entirely driven out of her head all thoughts of the Dale connection that might have been. And, to do her justice, she had been brought up to believe what she was told, and long repetition had inclined her to take Lily's frequent denials of any but a sisterly interest in Mr. Eames at face value.

"Such rapid progress in winning the affections of a lady," said Lily, "is not what I should have expected of Mr. Eames."

Now Lily would strongly have denied that there could possibly be any trace of anything resembling asperity in her voice at that moment. Grace, however, could not be quite so sure. Throughout that day she noticed – or thought she noticed, for Grace was nothing if not strictly just in her observations – a little terseness, a slight shortness of temper in her friend. Perhaps it was her headache still troubling her? It did seem to be persisting, if the pained expressions which found their way onto Lily's face were anything to go by. And yet... Grace would not quite swear that the headache seemed to return every time she mentioned her cousin. She could not be strictly accurate as to every case. But it certainly appeared so.

When Lily refused to go out that evening, Grace was quite sure that something was amiss.

"Is there anything wrong?" she asked. "Should we send for a doctor?"

"There is nothing wrong with me. Why should you think there is anything wrong with me? That is to say, I have been feeling a little out of sorts, and I do not care to go out tonight. But as to any more than that, you need not be alarmed. Please make my excuses to Mr. Kornhopper and his daughter. Bernard will understand, I am sure."

Grace said no more, comforting herself that Dr. and Mrs. Crofts would be with them shortly. Lily would surely speak more freely to her own sister, and if there was anything in the medical line to be done, she could have no better advice than that of Dr. Crofts.

Left to herself that evening, Lily found she had ample leisure to contemplate the situation. Mr. Eames, was, of course, of no concern to her, merely an old, childhood friend, and she could have no part in any choice of his future wife other than to wish him joy. What right, then, did she have to feel so bereft? Many times she had told him that her dearest wish was to see him happily married. Why, then, should the prospect of such an event have this effect on her? Was a man never to have any happiness in his life simply because she had refused him?

In her own way, Lily was every bit as intelligent as her friend Grace, but it had still not quite occurred to her that perhaps it was not Mr. Eames's happiness she was concerned about, but her own.

Chapter Seventeen

IS HE OR ISN'T HE?

By Monday morning, Lily had decided that she was not justified in ignoring her social obligations any longer, whatever the state of Mr. Eames's marital prospects. Such prospects, indeed, were a matter of the most extreme indifference to her, and she owed it to her friend Grace to take as much delight in any good news as she could. She resumed, therefore, her daily round of calls and visits.

It was on the way through the park to call upon Lady Glencora that the true state of this indifference began to dawn upon her. Strictly speaking, of course, it was not really necessary to go through the park on the way from the Bishop's to the Pallisers', but it was such a delightful morning and both young ladies, for their own reasons, thought that a walk in the fresh air might be a good thing in the circumstances.

After a period of inclement weather such as had occupied the weekend, it was delightful to be walking in the fresh air of a beautiful spring morning. The sun was bright, but not blinding. The air was warm, but not enervatingly so. The grass seemed greener for its refreshment, and the flowers lent an enchanting touch of colour to their carpet.

Grace had been remarking upon a particularly beautiful rhododendron when, rounding a bend in the path, she caught sight of her cousin.

"Look, Lily, there is Johnny, by the lake. And who is that lady walking with him? Could it be Miss Palliser, do you think?"

However confused she might be, Lily was in no doubt about her courage.

"There is an easy way to find out," she replied. "I am sure we are justified in asking for his news."

And her back seemed straighter, and her step firmer than of late, as she led the way.

"How nice to see you back, Mr. Eames. London has not been the same in your absence. I trust your visit was satisfactory, and that the nation's finances are now on a firmer footing?"

This was not the way that Johnny was used to being addressed by so old a friend.

"The nation's finances," he replied, "are in safer hands than mine, I do assure you. But, yes, my time at Matching was productive, or at least I think so, and I believe Mr. Palliser would agree."

"Surely there can be no doubt about that," said his companion. "and it was not all work, you know. Do not tell me that there was nothing at Matching beside your labours which gave you even a little pleasure. But do introduce me to your friends, Mr. Eames."

"Some things, as you might guess, gave me a great deal of pleasure. But I am sorry, I have been remiss. Please allow me – my cousin Mrs. Grantly and my oldest friend, Miss Dale. Mrs. Grantly, Miss Dale, Miss Claudia Palliser."

"Any relation to Bishop Grantly?"

"Major Grantly, my husband, is Bishop Grantly's son."

"My cousin Plantagenet thinks very highly of the Bishop. I must call on you while I am in town. And Miss Dale? Would that be from Allington, now?"

"My cousin Bernard is the present squire."

"Just so, I met Mrs. Bernard Dale only last week at Matching. An enchanting person, like all Americans. But I believe her father is immensely rich. You must all come to call at Park Lane. Do not stand on ceremony. My cousin is always pleased to see anyone I invite."

"We were on our way to Lady Glencora's just now. We see each other almost every day."

"Then we must go there immediately. I am so pleased to be of service to you, Miss Dale. Mr. Eames had told me so much about you."

In truth, the name of Lily Dale had never passed Johnny Eames's lips while he had been at Matching. Miss Palliser, however, had a fine talent for spotting a potential rival, and an instinctive way of putting all such down. With this in mind, she took charge of the party and led the way to the gate that led to the little passage to the town house of the dukes of Omnium. The narrowness of this path necessarily led to a separation of the party into two pairs, or, perhaps, in one person's mind at least, into two couples.

Lily, as she followed, could not tell herself with any degree of honesty that her mind was at rest.

She had scarcely spoken two words uninterrupted to Mr. Eames since they had met, and now to walk behind him while Miss Palliser clung to his arm and seemed to usurp his every step was not congenial. This behaviour of Miss Palliser seemed so very, very proprietorial. What right had she to commandeer Mr. Eames in such a manner? Unless, of course, cousin Arabella had been right. That could not be, naturally. Certainly it could not be. The undying love of Johnny Eames for Lily Dale was the one fixed constant in a changing universe. And yet... and yet.

In her anxiety, Lily did not reflect that Miss Palliser's manner was universally proprietorial. She had taken Mr. Eames in hand just as she had taken upon herself to invite Lily and Grace to her cousin's house. She had taken charge of the party simply because she was a Palliser, and that was what Pallisers did. She did not stop to consider that there might be any other way.

Likewise, Lily did not stop to consider the likelihood of the situation. It seemed to her that this man she had always thought of as somehow her own was now lost to her, and she found that she could not help grieving.

She scarcely noticed where she was until she found herself seated in lady Glencora's parlour.

It then became absolutely necessary that she should take part in the conversation, though the part she played was a rather shabby one, badly-scripted and worse acted. Her random answers and general air of listlessness brought forth renewed enquiries about her health.

This at length induced her to remember her headache and to beg to be allowed to retire.

Lady Glencora was all solicitation, but would not hear of the girls returning through the park on foot on such a hot day and with Lily in such a condition. A carriage should be fetched to convey her the two streets distance. In the meantime, let Grace hasten back to prepare her friend's bed and any other necessities. Mr. Eames would escort his cousin, of course, and perhaps Claudia would keep them both company?

Lady Glencora, as always, was universally kind, and, as always, she got her way, and in a very few moments Lily found herself alone with her ladyship.

"Now, my dear," said Lady Glencora "I could see that something was troubling you and you did not want to talk in company. Now, tell me all about it."

"My headache…" Lily began.

"Oh, headaches! I know all about these headaches, and I wager I know the cause of this one. You are not best pleased with the way my cousin treats Mr. Eames, is that not it?"

For answer, Lily surprised herself again by bursting into copious tears.

Lady Glencora took her in her arms.

"There, there, my dear. I see it all now. But didn't they tell me that you had already refused Mr. Eames ever so many times?"

"Oh, Lady Glencora, I have been such a fool! What am I to do?"

"Well, it seems to me that that depends a great deal upon what Mr. Eames does. But I will tell you what I think he will not do. He is not going to marry my husband's cousin Claudia."

"But....."

"But me no buts. I have seen the way she has been throwing herself at him and I have seen the way you have taken it. But I will tell you what else I have seen. I have seen the way he has taken it. I suppose I should not say this but the Honourable Miss Claudia Palliser is not a very great adornment to our family. Her father spent what little money he had, and his daughter has been trying to marry for more ever since. She made a determined effort for Mr. Eames down at Matching. I had a word with her myself about that, and Mr. Palliser had a word with Mr. Eames, and we both thought the thing was settled, but it appears that she has not yet given up. But at any rate, Mr. Eames told my husband that it was out of the question that he should harbour any matrimonial intentions towards Claudia as his affections had long been engaged elsewhere."

"But that only means that it is not Miss Palliser. There may be someone else."

"Dear Lily, if you think that, then you really are a goose, and I can't say that I have ever noticed anything particularly anaticulous about you before. There! I am learning long words out of the dictionary to please Planty, and I never thought I would get that one into a conversation. But, seriously, I really do not think you need concern yourself, although, from all the encouragement you have ever given the young man, it would jolly well serve you right if he did marry someone else."

"I have often told him to do just that," was Lily's reply to this.

"But did you mean it?"

"I thought I did, but I was young then. Now..."

"Now?"

"Forgive me, Lady Glencora, I cannot persuade myself that you are right. But now, just now, I find I am not so sure of anything as I once was."

Chapter Eighteen

REUNIONS

Lily's reflections upon the exact nature of the understanding between Mr. Eames and Miss Palliser could not be of long duration, for the following morning a message arrived from Barchester.

The Crofts had decided to bring forward their visit to London and expected to arrive that very day, in time for a late dinner.

It was imperative that their lodgings should be prepared for them. These were in a most respectable house in Curzon Street, where a very spacious apartment, capable of accommodating both Dr. and Mrs. Croft together with Lily, had long been bespoken by the Bishop. Dr. Grantly had not shirked in carrying out this task, which had been wished upon him by his visitors, although at first he had been much averse to the plan. Indeed, it was his earnest desire that Lily should remain in his house and that her sister and brother-in-law should join her there. There would have been ample room, more than ample room, and they were all good friends, were they not? Seven or eight at the breakfast table was no great crush, surely?

And what did a little waiting for bathrooms and such signify? He yielded, however, to Dr. Croft's insistence that he should have his own place while in the capital, and, having undertaken the duty, performed it admirably.

The apartment was said to be fully furnished and fitted out. Those less familiar with these matters might therefore have supposed that the proprietors would provide all that was necessary and that the party from Barchester would have nothing to do but unpack when they arrived and commence their metropolitan existence. Lily and Grace, of course, knew better. What, trust to a London landlord for the cleanness of the floors and furniture, not to mention airing the beds and linen? These things must be seen to personally, and there must be fires and food waiting to welcome the newcomers on their arrival.

In one matter the bishop did prevail. Lily and Grace, remembering their days in the Small House and at Hogglestock Parsonage, and totally unmindful of the necessary dignity of their current positions, were quite capable of lowering themselves, both literally and metaphorically, by getting down on their hands and knees to scrub the floors themselves,. The Bishop's scandalised insistence, however, that he had an ample staff available to perform these menial tasks and that the young ladies should limit themselves to supervision met with no great resistance.

Even so, it was quite impossible that such supervision could be exercised lightly, or even by proxy, as the elder Mrs. Grantly had suggested.

Nothing would do but that Lily should be on the spot to make quite certain that everything was just so. And as Lily was to be there all day, then Grace must go too.

In fact, the rooms were already tolerably clean – remarkably so, for a rented flat - the gas lights functioned, the water was turned on, the furniture was adequate, and there was really very little wanting apart from the aforementioned airing and the preparation of a meal. The domestic staff hired with the apartment could not be provided until the following day, and at first it seemed that there would indeed be actual work to do. But in fact both these tasks were already spoken for by the bishop's cook and housekeeper, and so the two young ladies found themselves engaged in arranging flowers on the sideboard and with ample time on their hands for conversation.

In these circumstances, the subject of Mr. Eames inevitably arose.

"Is it not strange," asked Grace, "that Cousin John should be keeping his engagement secret from us? What can his reason be?"

"I dare say Miss Palliser's grand relatives are not impressed by her marrying a clerk from an office and they do not wish to risk offending them as yet –if, indeed, there is such an engagement."

"How could there not be, when the lady as good as told us so herself? And, Lily, you know John is not exactly an ordinary clerk."

"No, he is not, is he? Not now, not for a long time, I think. I remember calling him that many years ago when mother and Bell and I were talking about... we were discussing someone else, and mother told me that he would yet make his mark in the world. Well, he has made it now, and is well on the way to making a greater one, and I am still what I said I would remain- Lily Dale, Old Maid."

"Oh, Lily! As if you would ever be an old maid!"

"But I am one, and I begin to see what it is to live so. You have your Henry, your little ones to come, all your life still ahead of you. My life is all behind me. I lived it all in those few weeks before the man I was engaged to found that an earl's daughter would be more desirable a connection than a mere gentleman's. Now Bell has her own life, mother lives only for Bell, and what have I to comfort myself with? Nothing but the knowledge that I have been true to the Dales?"

"Lily, dear Lily, this is not like you. I expected more from you, who have ever been to me the very pattern of cheerful confidence. I have always thought that your pride in your family and your name was your chief source of joy, and I have often wondered whether such emotions are truly Christian. But I have also considered that I did not know you before.... before your misfortune. Lily, dear, are you sure that you have not let that man ruin your life?"

"I have no need of a man to do that. I am perfectly capable of acting on my own behalf."

"My father would say that that sounds rather like the mortal sin of despair."

"Your father is a very good man. We cannot all hope to live up to him."

"But, Lily, what is it you want?"

"I do not know. I am sure I wish Johnny Eames every happiness. But I have always thought of him as somehow different from other men. Perhaps the knowledge that he is much the same as others ought not to grieve me, but the truth is that it does."

This sort of conversation was not pleasing to either of the participants, and there is no telling how long it might have continued, had it not been interrupted by the arrival of Doctor and Mrs. Crofts, both much fatigued from their journey. The welcoming of the new arrivals, and the installing them in their new quarters which followed proved a welcome distraction, and soon thereafter the family sat down to dinner well contented, or, at least, a superficial observer would have said so.

"My father-in-law," said Grace, "wanted to have you round to dinner tonight, but we persuaded him that the last thing you would want to do after such a journey would be to go into society. Indeed, I feel that I am imposing myself upon what would otherwise be really a family party."

"Not at all," replied Doctor Crofts, "I am sure Lily thinks of you quite as a sister, and what Lily thinks, Bell thinks, and what Bell thinks, I think. There! So, you see that we are all family here."

"You are too kind, sir. But, before I forget, Bishop Grantly begs that you will do him the honour of dining with him tomorrow night, if you are not previously engaged."

"Please tell the Bishop that the honour will be ours. I must go to the Royal College in the morning, but my afternoons are quite at my disposal, as are my evenings as yet."

"Mark the 'as yet', my dears," said Bell. "As an old married woman I can tell you it is the sign of a gentleman who expects to be busy in the days to come, and is already preparing his excuses for neglecting his poor, devoted wife."

"But you would not want me to neglect the opportunities this visit gives me to improve my professional standing, would you dear? I really must spend some time with the faculty now that I am here, although we now have a few days in hand. And you will always have Lily for company."

"I would not have you neglect your opportunities, dear, but I do expect you to pay due regard to your family. Lily will be the best of helps and comforts, but I also expect to see more of you than breakfasts and suppers, you know."

"Which reminds me," put in Lily, wishing to smooth over what she perceived as an apparent sign of friction between her sister and the Doctor, " I must pack my traps and give notice to the poor, dear Bishop that I am quitting him. He so loves having a full house. He will be sorry to lose a guest, even one as inconsequential as I am."

"He will not be the only one who will miss you, Lily," said Grace.

"I will miss you, too, my dear, but we are just round the corner, you know, and Major Grantly's business at the Horse Guards is almost finished, and, to tell you the truth I will be rather glad to be away from such constant intercourse with Park Lane. Mr. Palliser and Lady Glencora are very kind, but it will do me good to descend from the stratosphere for a while. And there are other members of their set whom it will be just as well I should avoid for a while."

This was a subject on which Grace did not wish to proceed further, and she was glad to turn the conversation by enquiring after the health of Mrs. Dale.

"She has been feeling rather out of sorts lately." said Bell. "So much so that I persuaded her to consult Frederick. But she insisted that we should come as we had arranged, and leave her with the children, so I am persuaded that there is nothing seriously wrong. I am sure that she would have told me if there were, or that Frederick would have done so."

"I assure you, my dear, that if any immediate cause for alarm existed you would know about it."

The rest of the evening passed in the way such reunions do, in talk of matters whose interest, though great in itself, was of importance only to a very small circle.

It was arranged, as they were all to dine at the bishop's the following evening, that Lily would postpone her removal to Curzon Street until the day after.

Doctor Crofts escorted the two ladies on the short walk back, but declined to come in, pleading the fatigue of the journey and an indisposition to leave Bell alone for too long in a strange place.

"Well, my dears," said Susan Grantly as they entered the parlour, "And how are Doctor and Mrs. Crofts? Are they nicely settled in, and shall we see them tomorrow."

"They are well, they will soon be comfortable

and they thank you for your kind invitation and accept it with pleasure," said Lily.

"Good, good. I am sure the dear Bishop would like a word with the doctor. His lumbago, you know. Well, I am glad you had an amusing time in Curzon Street. You missed nothing here, to be sure, nothing but curates and chaplains all day. Oh, and Mr. Eames called, asking for you, Lily, but as I thought you would not choose to be interrupted I merely told him you were not at home."

Chapter Nineteen

MORE SCENES IN A MODERN PALACE

The Crofts, when they arrived the following afternoon at the palace of the Bishop of Westminster, thought at first that they had mistaken the address. Here was neither gothic spendour nor baroque opulence, but a plain door in a plain street of plain, if obviously substantial, houses. There was no hint of anything important, no trace of anything ecclesiastical, not so, much as a brass plate on the door, which was unadorned save for its number and the usual fittings.

Doctor Crofts, at least since his success in both marriage and his profession, was not a man much given to hesitation, but he thought it best to consult his wife before knocking.

"We did follow Lily's directions, did we not? And this is the number she said?"

"Five minutes on foot, she said, and that is how long we have been walking. And a brown door, number eighteen."

"Well, it is not exactly Barchester, is it? But we must try."

The knocker may have had nothing of sanctuary about it, but it was solid brass, and it performed its function. Scarcely had Doctor Crofts raised his hand from it than the door was opened by a person of distinctly clerical aspect, who brushed past them, saying,

"Do come in. You will find my lord Bishop at the end of the passage . And I hope you will find him in a more becoming mood than I left him."

Other greeting was there none, and the visitors were left to make their own way to the end of the corridor, where an open door on the right gave them a view of Doctor Grantly in the act of flinging down his pen."

His face brightened at sight of them, however, and he strode across the floor with hand outstretched.

"Doctor Crofts! And Mrs. Crofts. How delightful to see you. You must have come by the mews entrance."

"A clerical gentleman let us in," said Bell. "He seemed in some haste."

The smile left the bishop's face for a moment.

"Yes. That would be Doctor Snodgrass, the new archdeacon wished upon me by the evangelicals in parliament. Upon my word, archdeacons are not what they were when I was made one. To speak so to his own bishop...but let us not go into that. Shall we join the ladies?"

And, so saying, he led the way to a much more comfortable part of the house, indeed, to the drawing room, where they found Lily sitting with both Mrs. Grantlys.

"Susan, my dear," said the Bishop, "look who has done us the honour of calling at the tradesmen's entrance."

"Oh, dear," said Lily, " that was my fault I am afraid. I am so used to slipping in and out that way to get to Curzon Street that I never thought to give directions to the front of the house."

"Well, well, you are here now, so never mind that," said the bishop, "although we must take care to show you the grand portal in due course. Tell us all the news from Barchester – but first, you are dining with us tonight, are you not, which reminds me, we will be a gentleman short, I must do something about that..."

At this point the servant entered to announce Mr. Eames.

"Why the very thing!" Exclaimed the bishop. "Mr. Eames, you must dine with us tonight. It will just be a small, family party, only those you can see in this room, so there will be nothing grand, but you will rescue Miss Dale from the shame of being without a partner, which is a great consideration, you know."

"I would be delighted, my lord, but perhaps, as it is such a family party, I ought not to intrude."

"For shame, John!" said Bell. "Do you think that there is only Grace here who considers you to be part of her family?"

"I am only too aware of the great kindness which has been shown by both the Dales and the Grantlys to me and to my family. I try, therefore, not to trespass upon it."

"Very proper, I am sure, young man," said the bishop, "but I pray you not to refer to such things again. We are, as Mrs. Crofts has put it, all family here – in a sense, that is."

"In a sense, my lord, then so be it. But what sense, exactly, I will not dwell upon."

The conversation which ensued, although it may be assumed to have been of particular and abiding interest to those who had been fortunate enough to have been born in either Barchester or Guestwick, was not such as to impress its merits upon those not so blessed. Indeed, even to one of the participants, who had come fortified with rather more to say than the usual morning call commonplaces, and with a purpose more definite than the mere excision of fifteen minutes from the period before lunch, the gossip about Mr. This and Canon That which occupied the minds of his fellows was of less than compelling interest. Mr. Eames soon made his goodbyes, therefore, although not before promising to eat the bishop's mutton with him that evening.

"John seemed very preoccupied," said Grace privately to Lily.

"From all I hear, he has plenty to preoccupy him." was the rejoinder, in tones more tart than were wont to be used on the subject.

Grace could not help but mark this, but said nothing.

Dinner that evening, albeit a mere family affair, was still something of an occasion. Henry Grantly had returned at last from Paris, and it was his first night in London with Grace. Conversely, Lily was spending her last night at the bishop's before removing to Curzon Street. Such things have their own occult means of communicating themselves to the domestic staff and a special effort had consequently been made with the meal.

It might, however, have been bread and water, for all the company noticed. Henry and Grace were preoccupied with each other, and the Crofts had succumbed to that weariness which afflicts travellers when their journey is at last done. Who does not know that feeling? That deceptive light-heartedness to be at last out of the train or carriage, that elated rush of apparent energy which sets one off on a tour, it may be, of an entire new city, to be replaced so soon by the realisation that one is, perhaps, not really quite as young as one used to be, is something which all but a very few share.

The bishop and the elder Mrs. Grantly did their best to keep the conversation going, but it was evident that their task was a hard one.

Lily and Johnny found small talk difficult at first, and were reduced to enquiring after mutual acquaintances. After exhausting all the current scandals and the latest drolleries of Dolly Longstaff, it was inevitable that the name of Miss Claudia Palliser should occur.

"Lily," said Johnny, "there is something I must tell you about Miss Palliser."

Lily felt her heart stop.

"John," she said. "Take care. There is nothing you need tell me about that lady."

"But I think I must. I think, from certain things you have said lately, from other things you have done, that you have heard something about Miss Palliser and me. Words – I once thought something more than words – have passed between you and me in days gone by which I think entitle you to an explanation."

"John, you need never explain yourself to me."

"But I think I must. Indeed I must. I am aware that there are rumours circulating concerning Miss Palliser and myself, based on certain things that occurred when I was staying at Matching. I have not a word to say against Miss Palliser, but I would have you know that there is no truth in those rumours, none whatsoever."

"Then you are not....?"

"We are most definitely not engaged to be married, nor is there any likelihood that we ever shall be. I believe Miss Palliser is not averse to the match, but it takes two to make that sort of thing up, and I for one do not consider it possible that I could ever be a party to it. I told Mr. Palliser so when he thought it necessary to enquire after my attentions when we were at Matching. Lily, I would say this no man or woman living except to you, but between the two of us there must always be nothing but the truth."

Lily found herself once more capable of breathing, but totally incapable of carrying on any sensible conversation. She was somewhat relieved, therefore, when Mr. Eames' attention was engaged by an enquiry from the bishop as to the likelihood of the tenpenny shilling being introduced in his lifetime.

It was necessary, it was vital to think much upon what Johnny had said, to decide just why it was that the denial of his engagement should be so pleasant to her ears. If only she could talk to Grace about it. But, oh dear, Grace had been so pleased with the match. How disappointed she would be now! Whatever was to be done?

These ruminations, however, were shortly interrupted by the entry of a footman bearing a silver tray with a brown envelope.

"Pardon me, my Lord, but a telegram has come. For Miss Dale."

Chapter Twenty

MR. MORSE'S INVENTION

"A telegram has come."

How often have we heard those words? Too often, I dare say. And how often have we thrilled to hear them? Far too seldom, I rather fear. No doubt Mr. Morse, and Sir Samuel Wheatstone before him, felt that they were bestowing a great new benefit upon mankind, but how many of us have appreciated that benefit? Oh, in business, no doubt, and in politics, such rapid communication has its attractions. But we are not all stockbrokers waiting on the latest news of the markets, and still less are we statesmen or generals waiting to tell the world of our latest conquest in one well chosen word in a dead language. For a private person, a telegram, nine times out of ten, is news that we do not want to hear, all too often news that means getting out our black coats and funereal ribbons, and thinking on things we would rather not.

This was the kind of thought which immediately struck all the party, and Lily's hand was shaking as she took up the silver paper knife.

"Please, my dear," said the bishop, "use no ceremony, I beg you. We will all attend to our mutton while you are engaged."

Nevertheless, Lily felt that all eyes were upon her when she slit the envelope.

This was only natural, since the eyes of all the party were upon her, and what they saw only confirmed them in their forebodings.

Lily's face turned the colour of the tablecloth, and her hand went to her mouth.

"I must go," she cried. "I must go at once." and she was immediately making to rise from the table.

"My dear," exclaimed the bishop, "whatever is the matter?"

Lily passed the paper to Doctor Crofts.

"Read it," she said. " I cannot bear to."

Doctor Crofts unfolded the paper, which Lily had crumpled into a ball.

"Mrs. Dale seriously ill," he read. *"Come at once. Jenkins."*

"Dr. Jenkins," he said, "is my locum. He is a competent man, and would not alarm us needlessly."

With a muffled scream, Bell slid to the floor in a swoon.

The ensuing confusion need not be described. How often, dear reader, have you been at dinner in the house of a prominent cleric when a female guest has fainted and another is crying out for a carriage, while all around are struck both dumb and motionless with shock and horror? If you are familiar with situations of the sort, you need no such description. If such familiarity has not come your way, it needs little imagination to supply the want.

Amid all the cries for water, for brandy, for

smelling salts, all the fanning of faces and chafing of hands, no one noticed that Mr. Eames had left the room until he returned with another ominous yellow envelope.

"I took the liberty," he said, "of sending a servant round to Curzon Street to ask if they had had a telegram for Mrs. Crofts. Here it is. I make no doubt that it contains much the same news. Doctor Crofts, how soon can you and Mrs. Crofts be ready to return to Barchester?"

Doctor Crofts looked up from where he was kneeling on the floor ministering to his wife.

"We meant to make the announcement later this evening." He said. "Mrs. Crofts is in an interesting condition. We are expecting another addition to our family. With this news I fear the worst. We must get Bell to bed and she must rest for at least another day before any travel will be possible."

"In that case," said Mr. Eames, "Lily, I take it that you will want to start at once. The night mail leaves at eleven forty-five and gets into Barchester at four fifteen. I have sent your maid to pack your overnight things and there is a cab waiting outside. There should be a few minutes to spare."

"My word, young man," said the bishop, "you have taken much upon yourself."

"He has kept his head," said Henry Grantly, "which is more than the rest of us have done. But are you seriously proposing that Miss Dale should travel alone on the night mail to Barchester?"

"Not alone," replied Johnny, "I will accompany her and be her escort. I am familiar enough with the night mail to Barchester, and I will telegraph my office not to expect me tomorrow. I am also familiar enough with Miss Dale, I hope, that she will not find objections to such a proposal."

"Oh, John," said Lily, "whatever should we do without you?"

"Never mind that. Run and finish your packing. Hurry or we shall miss the train."

After Lily had left the room, Johnny turned again to Doctor Crofts.

"Had you any reason to fear for Mrs. Dale when you left Barchester?" he asked. "Not that I expect anything anti-Hippocratic from you, of course, but, was she ill in any way?"

Doctor Crofts adopted the grave expression so often seen on the faces of members of his profession.

"Mrs. Dale has been ill for a long time," he said. "She did not wish her daughters to know and I have been constrained to keep it a secret from them. Now at last it is out we may be able to adopt more efficacious methods with the disease. But it is a malady which might have gone on for years without any more signs than a gradual lowering of the constitution. Had I expected a sudden turn for the worse I would not have left her in Barchester. I say this because I genuinely believe it, not because I merely want to believe it. To tell you the truth, this sudden collapse does concern me. It may be Jenkins covering himself against charges of negligence, but I doubt it. I should never have thought that of him. I cannot say more without examining the patient, but the prospects do not appear good to me. You will note that I do my best to maintain a professional calm, but it is not without some very great effort. Look after Lily, and I will do my best to look after Bell. We will join you as soon as we can."

"I will," said Johnny, "I will look after Lily."

Five minutes later, both were gone into the night.

Chapter Twenty-One

DARK DAYS

The news from Barchester the following morning came in a telegram addressed to the bishop, which arrived as these things do, just as the family were sitting down to breakfast. Doctor Grantly was a gentleman normally fond of his porridge and kedgeree, but he felt his appetite fail at the first words.

"I must go round to Curzon Street," he said. "Perhaps the ladies would care to accompany me?"

And he handed round the telegram for all to read.

The message was from Johnny, who had adopted this means of breaking the news to Bell as gently as possible, narrowly intercepting a direct missive from the good Doctor Jenkins to his employer. More details were promised in a letter to follow, but the full weight of the news could not be avoided. Mrs. Dale, good, patient, kind Mrs. Dale, who had borne so much all her life so that her daughters might have to bear the less, was no more.

Strange as it might seem, Bell took the news more calmly than her friends had expected. It was as if the previous night's collapse had used up all her emotions for the moment.

"Poor Lily," she said, "to have gone so far and all in vain. We must go to her at once."

Her husband, who was for once more alarmed by such stoicism than by any display of feminine weakness, represented to her that her condition did not permit of such rapid transitions, but he did so with no real conviction, knowing all along that it was now impossible for them to remain in London. All his solicitude and his reasoning could affect against female insistence was his wife's reluctant consent that instead of rushing at once to the station they should depart the following day, by a comfortable train, at a reasonable time, after they had informed all those concerned and cancelled all their commitments .

The full news came by an express letter later that day.

"We arrived," wrote Johnny, *"in the fag end of the night, worn-out and anxious. Mrs. Dale was conscious, and in no apparent pain. Doctor Jenkins and Mr. Crawley were with her. She asked for a few moments alone with Lily, so we left them together. Not five minutes later, we heard Lily cry out, and rushed back. She was sitting there, the tears running down her poor face, her arms round her mother's lifeless corpse.*

"The archdeacon has been a tower of strength, and has put all necessary arrangements in train. Lily has scarcely said a word since. I used to think she was low after that man treated her so shamefully, but it is far worse now. She needs her family. Above all, she needs Bell."

So it was to drawn curtains and a house of

mourning that the Crofts returned to Barchester. Lily they found prostrate, and Johnny at his wits' end.

"I have never seen her like this before," he said. "She walks about the house, she sits at table, she murmurs indistinct commonplaces to the callers - there have been many – and when they have gone she sits and stares at nothing. Not a word save to a direct question and then no real answer. She eats nothing, she drinks next to nothing, I doubt if she sleeps. What are we to do?"

"Perhaps after the funeral?" suggested Doctor Crofts.

"The funeral, yes, well, I have telegraphed Bernard Dale, who is on his way. He will want her to be buried at Allington, I have no doubt, and it is only right. I never knew her husband, but he lies there, and old Christopher Dale who was so kind to me. But until we know for certain we cannot arrange anything. Transporting the.... The necessary transport will take time to arrange, right across Barsetshire, and with the hot weather coming on we cannot delay much longer."

At this point they were interrupted by the arrival of another telegram.

"Excuse me," said Johnny, "although I dare say I know...yes. Mr. Palliser sends almost daily with condolences and enquiries after my health and Lily's, but I know that it is also meant as a gentle reminder that I am wanted in London. But here I am, keeping you standing about in your own hall. You will want to see her – both of them. Bernard arrives tomorrow, and then there will be purely family affairs to settle in which I can have no part. I return to London the day after, but let me know when the ceremony is to be, and I will run down directly to Allington. In the meantime I am at Plumstead if needed. Her sister is what Lily needs at the moment. I am very glad you are here."

And so it was. The days that ensued followed their own inexorable course, the arrival of Bernard and Arabella, the mournful procession right across the county and beyond, the night at Allington with the coffin in the great hall – almost a lying in state – the words of praise and comfort from neighbours and friends, meant, no doubt, sincerely, but ringing so hollow and empty at such a time. What need is there to say more? If you have experienced such a time, dear reader, you will know all too well what pains and troubles it brings. If you have not, then you have been fortunate indeed. But your luck will not last. Such trials – aye, and greater, come to all of us in time.

But a better pen than mine has consigned the dwelling on pain and misery to others. Such times have to be gone through, and when they are over, gradually, just as the black gives way to the grey and then to everyday colours, so life resumes its normal course.

Not so for Lily, however.

"She blames herself," wrote Grace to her cousin John. " She believes that if she had been here she could somehow have prevented what happened, that she could have done something, that her mere presence at Barchester would have affected a cure for what has since been established to have been a cancer, or alternatively that her absence in London brought on the crisis. All this while admitting – no, insisting, that no-one could possibly have taken better care of her mother than Bell. It is nearly six months now and there has been no improvement. She never goes out. She takes no part in anything. Almost, she only speaks when spoken to. Her appetite has not returned, and she has become quite thin and pale. Mrs. Quiverful was here the other day and said that she had hardly recognised the bonny girl from Allington the last time she visited the Doctor's. We none of us know what to do with her, and I know Doctor Crofts gets very impatient. They are all going up to London again in a month's time, for Doctor Crofts to have a second attempt to read his paper to the Royal College. The hope is that the distractions of town will bring her out of herself. I wish I could believe it. I know you will do your best, dear John, but I have never seen a girl so obviously in a decline."

Chapter TwentyTwo

MR. EAMES IS BUSY

It has been said that it was some six months after the death of Mrs. Dale before the Crofts and Lily returned to London.

During that period, Johnny Eames had not been idle. For the moment, he emulated the Italian comedy, and was the servant of two masters. His superiors, both Mr. Palliser and Sir Raffle, seemed determined to make up for his previous independence by making of him a slave of their purposes alone. This, perhaps, was just as well, for he had begun to notice the recurrence of thoughts and feelings he had thought long dead, and it was no doubt for the best that he was given no time to brood upon them. There were no more mornings walking in the park, no more trips down to Barchester or Guestwick, no pleasant country house weekends. Instead he toiled industriously at his tasks, so much so that those concerned began to notice.

"Eames has matured at last," said Sir Raffle Buffle to his colleague Mr. Optimist. "I always thought he had it in him, you know, and my good friend Earl de Guest was of my mind – look at how he left him all that money. But there was always something lightweight about him. He always would go his own way, don't you know, and that won't do in an office such as ours. But now I see that he has come to my way of thinking, and I am sure there are great things in store for him. Old Brockenback is retiring shortly, isn't he? A word from me in the right quarters will no doubt be heeded."

"I really do not know what I should have done without Mr. Eames," was Mr. Palliser's comment to Lady Glencora. "Without him, these figures would never have been ready on time to present to the committee, and they prove my case conclusively, that the income tax would be a great deal easier to compute and assess with decimal currency. He has been invaluable."

"Something must be done for him," said Lady Glencora. "He has had a sad time, you know, with Miss Dale."

"Oh yes, a sad business, Mrs. Dale dying like that, just before we were due to meet Miss Dale's sister. Eames behaved perfectly correctly of course, and got back to work as soon as could be. He really has been invaluable. I shall mention him to the Prime Minister."

Johnny, meanwhile, was quite unaware of making himself indispensible to those in high places. The circumstances of Lily Dale's stay in London had led him to form a resolution, or rather to resurrect an old resolution he had thought long dead. On that last night at the bishop's, he had gone fully prepared to carry out his resolve. Then had come that fateful telegram. While others had doubted and hesitated, he had acted. He had done what was needed, knowing all the while that what he had set his heart upon could no longer be thought of, not for a great while at least. And now, from all the news from Barchester, that great while might well be extended to never. In his moments of leisure, he sometimes caught himself thinking that the next time he went to Allington would probably be for another funeral. Moments of leisure, therefore, he sought to avoid, and his success in doing so was so marked that many of his old friends were unaware that he was still in the capital.

He received final news of the impending visit in another letter from his cousin Grace.

"Doctor Crofts," she wrote, "has at last been invited again to regale the Royal College of Physicians with the fruits of his experience. I must confess I feel more than ever an ignorant girl when he talks of his theories, but I am sure it is all very learned and his colleagues will value him much for it. It has fallen out rather awkwardly, in a way, as Bell cannot travel in her condition. (She is thriving, by the way, in case what I have just said should give you any alarm for her.)

But in another way it is just as well, for Lily is to go to keep house for him, and we all hope that the occupation will divert her mind from the course it has taken these past few months. I know you will see her and do your best to cheer her up. You will find her much altered."

Much altered she was. Johnny of course met

the train from Barchester with a cab ready waiting. His first glance at the couple who stepped down from the train made him think there had been a change of plan. The little old woman by Doctor Crofts' side gave him a start. Then she looked up, and he saw that it was, indeed, Lily.

"Johnny," she said. "How strange you look. I expect you are annoyed to have us back on your hands like this."

"Not at all," he replied. "Quite the contrary. There is nothing I would rather be doing at this moment than welcoming you to London.... unless it were to welcome you as more than a guest."

But his attempted sally quite failed to bring any response, and, in any case, it was necessary to talk practical matters with the doctor. Lily said not one word more until he left them in their rooms in Wigmore Street.

The doctor pressed him to stay to dinner, but, feeling that Lily was exhausted by the journey, he pleaded a prior engagement and left them to their unpacking. They were to dine with him the following night, and he promised to call in the morning.

"Do you know," he said to Conway Dalrymple over the port that evening, "for a moment there, I really thought I had seen a ghost, and that it was old Mrs. Dale. Lily has aged thirty years in the past six months."

Dalrymple knew, or thought he knew, all the history of the past dealings between his friend and Miss Dale, although he had never met the lady.

"I had thought of painting her as Rachel." he said, for Mr. Dalrymple had made his name with paintings of young ladies modelling scenes from the bible, "but perhaps now it will have to be Sarah. In any case, what is all this I hear about you and your seat on the board, and the next honours list?"

"I'm sure you can have heard nothing," said Johnny. "As far as I am concerned, there is nothing to hear."

Another month passed. Doctor Crofts and Mr. Eames both had their work to do, and their days were increasingly occupied. Lily, once she had set their establishment in order, had absolutely nothing to do. Neither the Pallisers, nor the Grantlys were in town. Onesiphorus Dunn called twice and Dolly Longstaff once. Both were appalled at the change in Miss Dale.

"I've seen it before." said Dolly. "Usually it comes of being unlucky in love. This one's had that and her mother dying on top of it. She'll not be long with us, unless someone can shake her out of it."

"Johnny Eames is the man for that," said Mr. Dunn.

"On past form, Siph, old man, Johnny Eames is particularly not the man for that. But I think I know who might do."

Dolly Longstaff's prescription for Miss Dale's ills arrived at Wigmore Street the following afternoon.

"Mr. Adolphus Crosby, mum," said the maidservant as she showed the gentleman in.

Mr. Crosby achieved what neither Mr. Eames nor Mr. Longstaff had done. He made Miss Dale sit up.

"Thank you, Maria. Please ask Doctor Crofts to join us as soon as may be convenient."

The silence after the door closed behind the servant was full of memories.

"Well, Mr. Crosbie," said Lily at length, "I little expected to see you here. To what do I owe this honour?"

Crosbie had of late become much accustomed to discomfort, and the slight wince he gave at these words was barely discernible.

"I heard that you were ill," he said. "That you were at death's door, in fact. I could not keep away."

"I thank you for your anxiety, Mr. Crosbie, though what concern of yours my health may be I have no idea. As for death's door, one better than I has gone through it since we last met, and I have no doubt her passing was hastened by sorrow."

"Lily, I grieved to hear of your mother's death, and I grieve still more at your distress. If only..."

"You have no right to affect this concern for my family, and even less right to call me by that name, Mr. Crosbie."

"Lily, please, you have a perfect right to despise me. But believe me when I tell you that I have not had a moment's peace since I wrote that hateful letter from Courcy Castle. I know that I threw away a pearl beyond price for a trumpery bauble. I know that I did wrong, both to you and to the other lady. But, Lily, I have never stopped loving you, not for one moment. Every minute of my waking life, every moment of my dreams you are there. Can I not make amends? Can I not comfort you now, can we not be as we were once?"

And he was positively on his knees before her, clutching the hem of her gown, making an explicit declaration, before she could rise from her chair.

Lily felt the blood rushing to her cheeks, and it was with relief that she heard the sound of approaching footsteps in the hallway.

"Frederick!" she called. "Please come in here for a moment." And she pushed Crosbie away from her, sending him sprawling at her feet.

The door at last opened, to admit, not Doctor Crofts, but Johnny Eames, closely followed by Maria.

"Beg pardon, mum," she said, "the doctor's not to be found, but here's Mr. Eames."

"Mr. Crosbie is just leaving," said Lily. "Please show him out."

Mr. Crosbie's position on the floor was not one of advantage. He cast one look at either, and it was hard to tell which showed the more hate or envy. He scrambled to his feet, made a gesture of a bow, and shuffled out.

Lily collapsed again into her chair.

"Insufferable man! How could he? How could he come here and expect.....oh, I don't know what he expected? How could I have once deceived myself so much?"

"I never liked him," said Johnny, "I thrashed him once, and I have a strong inclination to follow him and do it again."

"No, Johnny, no. He is not worth the trouble. We do not want you in the police courts again, although I own the temptation is strong. I dare say it is unladylike of me to admit it, however."

"I will forgive you. I only looked in to see how you were, and it appears to me that you have more colour in your cheeks than many a day past.

Perhaps we ought to be grateful to Mr. Crosbie. It is a lovely day out. Will you not come for a walk in the park?"

"Do you know, Johnny, I think it would do me good."

Chapter Twenty –Three

A WALK IN THE PARK, AND WHAT CAME AFTER

The day was, indeed, beautiful, and the warm air and bright sunshine seemed to bring new life. Whether it was the weather or simply the time of day, the park was full of people who knew Lily, or Johnny, or both. Many of them were good enough to compliment Miss Dale upon her improving health and to hope that it would continue.

"Upon my word," said Lily after the fifth such encounter, " I had not thought that people were so concerned. But of course it is mere politeness, and means nothing."

"Much of it is that, and politeness is, after all, what keeps society jogging along. But it is not all hollow. You must believe that there are those who take a real and deep interest in the state of your health, indeed, in everything that concerns you."

"Bell is always interested, of course, and Frederick, a little."

This was deliberately to misunderstand, but both parties were perfectly well aware of that. There was a time when Johnny would have taken the point further, but today he merely smiled and admired the ducks on the pond.

In the days that followed, Lily's recovery continued, helped by the daily exercise and the constant company of Mr. Eames. So constant was this company, in fact, that tongues began to wag once more.

"When are we to wish you joy?" asked Conway Dalrymple. "And when am I to meet the fair Miss Dale?"

"What would I know about joy?" was Johnny's reply. "And you must know that I will not have Miss Dale talked about in that way."

"My sincerest apologies, old chap. But you must know that it is in just that way that people are talking. Seriously, though, I have my Rachel painting to think about. When are you going to bring her to me?"

"I will mention the subject," said Johnny. "I make no promises, mind. Still less can I promise to buy any painting which may ensue. I would not wish you to waste your professional time and talents. "

"It will be my wedding gift to you," said Dalrymple.

"In that case you really will be wasting your time," said Johnny.

To Johnny's surprise, Lily did not turn down the suggestion out of hand.

"Mr. Dalrymple is quite famous. I saw that picture you have, of Jael and Sisera, and I have seen lots more of his work since, in museums as well as in private houses. But how can he want to paint me, when we have never met? How does he know I will be suitable?"

"He knows we are very old friends, and thinks it

will be a compliment to me. I will not say that painting is his business and he expects to make money out of it somehow. He paints lots of society ladies in biblical costume. He did Lady Glencora as the queen of Sheba just last month. And usually the society ladies end up buying the picture."

"He must know there is no danger of that with me. The proverbial church mouse is rich by comparison. But I have always been in favour of compliments to you, Johnny, as you know."

The sittings were a success. Miss Dale and Mr. Dalrymple, though very different from each other in background and upbringing, hit it off with each other from the beginning.

"She is the perfect sitter, you know," Dalrymple told Johnny one day. "She never fidgets, is never bored, never questions why the pose must be necessary. And yet she can talk when wanted. I begin to think this Allington of yours a branch of paradise on earth, and all its denizens angels, or at least demigods."

He did not mention the one particular demigod who played a large part in their conversations.

So, gradually, Lily began to lead a normal life again, and to be seen about town. Things began to go smoothly again, and continued so until three days before the date set for Doctor Crofts' return to Barchester.

That morning Lily's post contained an envelope with unfamiliar handwriting. On opening it, she found a cutting from a newspaper. There was no covering letter.

"Whoever can have sent this?" she asked.

"I should ignore it if I were you," said Doctor Crofts. "Anonymous letters are never meant to be pleasant to the recipient. Throw it straight in the fire."

But Lily's eye had already been caught by a familiar name in print.

"The upper echelons of society in our capital," she read, "have lately been graced, if such is the appropriate word, by the presence of a Mr. John Eames, a person hitherto unknown to the public except for one incident a few years ago. That incident, in which Mr. Eames was arraigned before the magistrates of Marylebone for a violent assault upon a fellow passenger in a train at Paddington station, has perhaps passed from the memory of many. It has apparently slipped the minds of those who ought perhaps to exercise more care in their recollections. Mr. Eames, it has been learnt by this journal, is expected shortly to be appointed to a most prominent position, a position for which he is, in our opinion, by no means suited. Apart from the incident referred to above, Mr. Eames' career has so far been completely undistinguished in any way save one. That distinguishing factor is one which the general public may perhaps consider not to be the most appropriate for a high government official. The fracas at Paddington station apparently involved a lady, and it is evidently to Mr. Eames' success with the ladies that he owes his continuing success in his profession. Apart from the lady of Paddington, his name has been linked with several others, and it now appears that he is shortly to announce his betrothal to the cousin of a very highly placed government minister indeed. We are loath to raise the cry of nepotism, but we are bound to ask the question, "What are this egregious young man's qualifications for the position to which he is to be promoted?" The answer, as far as we can see, is this. He has made himself, not useful to his masters, but amusing to his masters' female relations. Such are the ways of the government which has now been oppressing this deluded nation for three years."

"How dare they?" cried Lily. "How dare they? The lady of Paddington, indeed! Oh, I will never forgive John Eames for this. And this "cousin of a highly placed government minister"! It can only be Miss Palliser. And after all he said! How could he be so false?"

"You know what they say about never believing anything you read in the newspapers. This is mere innuendo, and directed, I think, at Mr. Palliser. Our friend is merely a stick to beat him with."

"But there must be something in it. It would be actionable else, surely. Oh, to think of him coming courting here, with all his faithful Grizelda airs, and all the while he was engaged to that woman."

"I think you do John Eames an injustice, my dear. I think he is the least likely of all men we know to indulge in that sort of thing. And as for this...article, it is at most gossip, and none can know better than you how wrong mere gossip can be."

"Perhaps I was beginning to think favourably of what you call gossip. I almost think I was.

Perhaps.... But now, no, just wait. Just wait till I see him again and tell him what I think of him. Oh, I am sick of London. When can we go home?"

Mr. Eames was to dine with Doctor Crofts and Lily that evening, along with his cousin Grace, who had just arrived on a visit to the Bishop's. This threatened interview could not, therefore, be long delayed. The doctor was not one given to meddling. His professional experience had taught him that leaving well alone was usually the best treatment for any ill, whether of body or mind. In this case, however, he could not help thinking that the circumstances might excuse some interference. The time had almost come, he thought, when he would be obliged to act. In this mood, he awaited the evening's outcome as he would the crisis of a fever.

The dinner party could not be said to be a success. Grace and the doctor did their best, but Lily barely said two words from the arrival of the guests onward. Johnny seemed infected with her mood and was also unusually silent.

When the ladies rose to leave, Lily turned to Johnny.

"I would be obliged, Mr. Eames, if you did not linger over your port. There is something I particularly wish to say to you."

With such encouragement there could be no long conversation between the two gentlemen. Doctor Crofts thought he knew what was coming, and wondered if he should say a word or two to prepare Johnny for the storms ahead. But, then, what if there were no storms? Surely Lily was too sensible to be influenced by a scurrilous article in a cheap newspaper? And while the doctor was still making up his mind, Johnny had risen from the table.

"Shall we join the ladies, then, since they have something so particular in mind?"

The doctor, alas, had been over sanguine in hoping to avoid storms that evening. The tempest was in the air, and it broke in all its fury now around the head of Johnny Eames.

"Well, Mr. Eames, what have you to say to me?" asked Lily, with all the sweetness of a basilisk.

"What have I to say to you? Why, merely that I am very glad to see you looking so much better. The colour is quite back in your cheeks now, if I may be forgiven a personal remark. But you said you had something to say to me?"

"Indeed I have, Mr. Eames, indeed I have. And as for my forgiving your making a personal remark, that is the least of the offences for which you should at this moment be asking, no, begging my forgiveness."

Johnny blinked.

"I am sorry if I have unwittingly caused you pain in any way. You know that it would have been unwitting. But tell me my offence, that I may amend it."

"This offence cannot possibly have been unwitting. It has been prolonged, it has been deliberate, it has been deceitful. How can you pretend not to know the cause for my resentment."

"Lily, you know that I would never do anything intentionally to hurt you. Has someone been slandering me to you?"

"You would never do anything to hurt me! How

could you? What am I to you that you should think your actions mean anything to me? But what am I to think, Mr. Eames, what am I to do, when every day you come courting me, yes, courting me, and all the time you are engaged to another woman ? Tell me, and tell me truly this time, when are we to wish you and Miss Palliser joy? When will you cease your imposition on a helpless girl."

And she thrust the newspaper cutting into his hand.

"Read that, and then tell me that you have acted honourably towards me."

Kind friends had not been wanting to bring the offending article to Johnny's notice. Indeed, there had been several others of like tenor. One glance was sufficient for him to recognise, and to understand.

"The press are always on the lookout for something to fill their columns. When they run out of true stories to tell, they make up their own. All they ask is a few shreds of truth as a foundation on which to build the most fantastic structures."

"And this, I am to believe, is a 'fantastic structure'? When all around me tell me of its truth, its inevitability? When the lady herself tells all she meets that the ceremony will not be long delayed?"

"I say nothing of the lady. Indeed, I have said nothing to the lady for many weeks. I am aware that my name has been linked with hers. There will always be those kind enough to make such links. I have told you in the past and I repeat it today, there is no truth in such a story."

"As for that, Mr. Eames, I begin to wonder

whether your notion of truth and mine bear much resemblance to each other."

As soon as these words passed her lips, Lily knew that she had at last gone too far. One look at the face of her lover was enough to convince her of that. Never before had she seen such an expression. It was not so much any particular emotion as a complete absence of anything at all. It was the face of a dead man, and it was with the slow but inevitable ponderousness of a reanimated corpse that Mr. Eames now rose from his seat.

"Excuse me, Miss Dale. Doctor Crofts, I beg you will forgive me, but I must leave now. I find myself indisposed. Thank you for your kind hospitality."

Doctor Crofts had a very fair idea of the nature of his friend's indisposition, but it was necessary to go through the motions of polite enquiry and courteous regret before the guest could be allowed to depart.

Neither the enquiry nor the regret were effective in soliciting the nature of Mr. Eames' indisposition, nor, indeed, anything but the necessity of his going. The one person from whom a word, perhaps, might even now have sufficed sat mute upon the sofa, and said no more.

The wind in the street smote cruelly from the north, and blew sheets of rain into the faces of the passers-by.

"Why, John," said Mary on his return to the Athenaeum, "you are wet through. You must get to bed quickly, before you catch your death."

"So I must," replied Johnny. " If you say so. But what is so wrong, I sometimes wonder, with catching one's death?"

Chapter Twenty-Four

LATE POST

"Lily," said Doctor Crofts to his sister-in-law the following morning, "I could not help noticing a failure last night of that improvement in your spirits in which we have all been rejoicing, and this morning you seem no better. Is there anything to your knowledge which has brought on this relapse, this want of spirits? I speak as a medical man as well as one who loves you dearly as a sister."

"Anything to my knowledge?" asked Lily,."There has certainly been something brought to my knowledge which has not been to my liking. Perhaps it has brought on this "want of spirits" as you call it, although I did not know that was a medical term. I confess that I believe my spirits to be much as they ever were."

"I think I know to what you refer, and I think you know my opinion on that score. I will say nothing of Mr. Eames now. I know all your family and friends have said much to you on that subject, and I know the effect it has had. But I think now I must speak to you of your mother."

"Of my mother?"

"Yes, and of the last few days before we left her

in Barset. I told you that I was quite easy in my mind when we left her. That was true, in so far as I did not think there was any urgent cause for alarm. But I have to confess that your mother's health had been a cause of concern for some time before then. Although there seemed to be no imminent danger, both Mrs. Dale and I knew that the end could not be very far distant. Your mother had already made her arrangements, and part of those arrangements was this."

From his pocket he now produced an envelope, addressed to "Miss Lily Dale." The sight of the handwriting, so dear and so familiar, brought a gasp to Lily's lips.

"Your mother gave me this letter the night before we left her. She made me promise to give it to you if anything were to happen to her while we were away. I gave her that promise, but I have not yet carried it out. I did not do so at first because I did not think it advisable given the state of your health. Since you have been so improved I have been waiting for the right time. I think that time is now. I do not know all the contents of this letter, but I must say that Mrs. Dale told me some of it. Perhaps I was wrong in keeping it for so long. Perhaps I am wrong in giving it to you now. But I think I must. I have thought long and hard on what to do for the best, and I am convinced that, for all our sakes, it must be read now, if ever."

"I know not whether to be more provoked or mystified," said Lily. "But give it to me now, at any rate, and I will try not to blame you too much."

"Take it, and believe that we all wish only for

your happiness. I would mention that I have also been waiting for Bell's advice. I received her letter this morning, and she agrees that now is the time. I will leave you now, but I will be in my study if you wish to speak to me again this morning."

Words cannot describe the feelings with which Lily looked upon the envelope in her hand. To have been all these months mourning a beloved parent, lost without a word, and now, suddenly to have, as it were, her last words presented like this. Lily was by no means inclined to indulge in maidenly vapours, but her hand shook as she broke the seal.

The sight of the familiar writing brought tears to blind her eyes. It was some moments before she could be calm enough to make out a word.

"My own darling Lily," she read,

"If you are reading these words, it must mean that we will never see each other more until we meet in the presence of our blessed Lord. The doctors tell me that I must not despair, that they have treatments yet to try, that their diagnoses may be wrong. I do not despair. I hope I do not despair. But I know I must prepare for whatever may happen, and when I think of the future the temptation to abandon hope is strong indeed. For myself I have regrets, but no fear. Leaving my darling girls is a matter for sorrow, but there can be no sorrow in being united once more with their beloved father. My feelings, then, are mixed, but there would be less of sorrow in them if I could know that both my daughters had happiness in store. About Bell my heart is easy. She is married to a good man, whom she loves, and who will do well. She could not, and, I think, does not ask for

more. But, Lily, my darling Lily, my heart comes near to breaking when I think what will happen to you when I am gone. "Lily Dale, Old Maid", you used to joke about signing yourself. Will it still be a joke when you really are old, my love? Will you still be able to laugh when your hair is grey and your back is bent, when your eyes and ears are failing and your hands have lost their cunning, when all around you have their own lives and there is no-one to share yours?

"There is nothing in this world so precious for a woman as the love of a good man. It makes her complete, it provides the other half of herself she did not know was missing. It is a treasure beyond price. I know, because I possessed that treasure for all too short a time. Dear Bell, too, knows the worth of her Frederick, and Grace of her Henry. Why should I cite more examples, when you must see all this for yourself?

"Lily, my love, it would have made my last moments happier if I could have known that you were as fortunate as Bell and Grace. And why should you not be? Why should you not find your other half? Why must all thought of such things be beneath your notice?

"This has been a subject which has been taboo between us for too long now, but in these my last moments on this earth, I can pretend no more. We both know that there is a man who has deserved your notice, if any man ever has merited a woman's regard. I have no time left for pretence, my love. We both know who I mean, and what my thoughts are about him. It may be that he will never come again. It may be that he has already found someone else. I

cannot believe it of him, but such things may be.

"But, Lily, if he should come again, if he does come again, I beg you, I implore you, from the grave, do not throw away your chance of happiness. If you think there is any chance at all, take it, take it with both hands, and let the mother who loves you beyond all things die happy in that hope.

"God bless you and keep you my darling."

The signature was somewhat smudged, but quite legible, and not at all wavering.

"What now?" thought Lily, "What now?"

Chapter Twenty-Five

BOTANY BAY

Johnny Eames, it has been shown, had retired from Dr. Crofts' dinner party in a state of mind which was less than satisfactory. On setting out for Wigmore Street, he had told himself that he had not changed the intention he had formed on Lily Dale's previous visit to the capital, and had allowed himself to hope that his project might at last have some prospect of success. The improvement in Lily's spirits, and the pleasure she seemed constantly to express in his company had given some cause for sanguineness, and he had dared to believe that there was a chance that, this time, his ship would come in. Now, however, he saw all his hopes founder on the rock of a pettifogging scandal sheet, a mere retailer of second hand gossip, a paltry rag that no-one of any account even read.

The old hobbledehoy Johnny would have retired into solitude for days on end, and brooded on the blackness of all things. The new cosmopolitan Mr. Eames turned up for work the following morning. He could not, however, be induced to share the enthusiasm of Mr. Palliser.

"But that was brilliant work in that latest report of yours, Eames. The Prime Minister was most impressed. He said what a pity it was that you had had to turn down the seat at Barchester, as you were just the sort we wanted in the house. He agreed with me that your services have been quite exceptional, and that we ought to show our appreciation."

Johnny made the usual "Too kind" noises in reply to this.

"Not at all," continued Mr. Palliser. "This is a serious business. Believe me, in a day or two it will be all settled and I think you will have some news that will please you."

"I thank you, sir, but I have long given scant regard to such matters."

"Too little regard, Eames. It will not do to scorn everything that the world appreciates, you know. But, in the mean time, can you help me with one more problem?"

The world that day seemed united in a conspiracy to console Mr. Eames.

"Well, Eames," said Sir Raffle on his entry into the boardroom, "I think you know how pleased we all are on the Board with your work. We have been looking about for some time for a means to express our satisfaction, and I think I can now put you in the way of something very good."

At this point he paused for the expected sounds of obligation. They were not forthcoming, which gave the pause a disappointingly artificial air.

"I said, Eames, that I can put you in the way of something very good, something very good indeed.

An appointment is shortly to be made at the highest level in the service, an appointment which brings with it great responsibility, but also great rewards. I have put your name forward, and it has been approved. And so, Mr. Eames, I am authorised to offer you the position of Commissioner for Taxes in New South Wales, responsible for the complete reform and oversight of the colony's taxation. I need hardly add that such an official will be one of the chief personalities of the colony, and that the financial rewards are considerable. You will be expected to take up your new duties as soon as possible, so I suggest you begin sorting out your affairs. Take the day off to do so."

"You are too kind, sir," replied Johnny. "I thank you for the day's leave, which I can certainly put to good use. But I must point out that I have not yet said whether I will accept this position."

"What? Not accept it? Not accept such great advancement, such a position as must be the ambition of any man when he joins a department such as this? Surely you cannot mean to refuse? Mr. Eames, I thought more of you – we all thought more of you than that."

"I have not said that I mean to refuse. Nor, however, have I said that I will consent. To uproot oneself and settle on the far side of the globe is not something to be undertaken lightly, as I believe even you will admit, sir. I have, as you said, Sir Raffle, affairs to arrange. I also have family and friends to consider and to consult. I must, with all respect, decline to give you an answer at the moment. I promise, however, to do so within forty eight hours."

"Well, Mr. Eames, you do surprise me. I thought that this was an offer such as any young man in your position would seize with both hands. But no doubt the young men of today are not what they were when I was young. Forty eight hours, you say? Very well, but you must know that posts such as this are not kept open at the whim of every applicant. I have no doubt that there are many other candidates who would be only too willing to fill the vacancy."

"I dare say you are right, Sir Raffle, but, as you just reminded me, this is my day off, and, if you will excuse me, I have things to do."

"Well, Mary," were his first words as he walked into the drawing room of the Albany flat, "how should you like to set up house in Botany Bay?"

"Botany Bay?" came the answer, in chorus, for Johnny had not noticed that his sister was entertaining a visitor. He now saw, to his surprise, that the chair by the window was occupied by Miss Dale.

"Botany Bay?" repeated Lily, looking up from her teacake. "Why should Mary wish to go there?"

"Wishes have nothing to do with it. I am to be transported there, like the convicted felon that I am, in the eyes of some, at least. They call it promotion, and give it a grand sounding title, but what it comes down to is comfortable exile. But forgive me, Mary, I did not expect to find you engaged. We will speak of this later. For now I must step round and see what advice Messrs. Swan and Edgar can give me on bushranger's outfits. Your servant Miss Dale."

And he was gone before either of the ladies could say more.

"Well," said Mary, "whatever was all that about?"

"We must go round to Park Lane," replied Lily, who had been discussing her regret for the previous night's "misunderstandings" with her oldest female friend. That the misunderstanding involved that friend's brother was perfectly understood by both ladies, and they did not consider it any obstacle to their friendship. Young ladies often have such feelings with regard to their friends and their brothers, and they mean no more than those other feelings they entertain of marriages between those same friends and those same brothers.

"We must go round to Park Lane," said Lily, "Lady Glencora will know."

But Lady Glencora did not know.

"No, my dears," she said, "I have heard nothing of any design to send Mr. Eames to the colonies. I know that Mr. Palliser had quite other plans for him. But he must know his own mind, and no-one can stop him going to New South Wales, or Van Diemen's Land, or wherever, if he should choose to go. Do you know of any reason he may have for wishing to leave the country?"

Mary and Lily looked at each other.

"I think I might," said Lily.

"Well then, my dear," said Lady Glencora, "tell me, and we shall see what we can do."

Chapter Twenty-Six

DECISIONS

Breakfast at the Adelphi the following morning was a strangely subdued affair. Mary found herself at a loss for subjects of conversation which did not involve either Lily Dale or the antipodes, or both, while Johnny had too much to exercise his mind upon without resorting to the meaningless commonplaces of the "What glorious weather for the time of year!" variety.

The arrival of the post forced each to feign some semblance of life.

Mary opened her small, scented envelope forthwith.

"It's from Lily," she said. "She wants me to go there to dinner tonight."

"I see," said Johnny, "and shall you go?"

"I should like to. Doctor Crofts is to be out at some scientific gathering, and Lily will be quite alone else. I would enjoy a nice, girls' evening. But of course I will not go if you do not wish it."

"Why should I not wish you to enjoy yourself? Go, by all means. We must be duly grateful for all these marks of attention from the Allington family."

Johnny's letters met with a gaze of apparent

loathing. There were two of them, each in thick, heavy envelopes, each embossed with an official crest.

"Well," he said. "These look as if they contain my fate, and I am strangely reluctant to tempt fate today. But I suppose I must open them."

And he did so, and spent, so it seemed to Mary, an unconscionable time reading them.

"Well?" she asked.

"This is the formal offer of the Australian post, which I must now answer formally. I shall not do so, however, until tomorrow, and perhaps not even then. But it seems that I must either give up all prospects of further advancement in the Department or else apply myself to taxing the squatters and convicts. I need to consider what alternatives there may be."

"And the other letter?"

"Oh, that is from Mr. Palliser, with a suggestion for one of those alternatives. I doubt if I will take it up. Mary, my dear, forgive me, but I need to think, and I am in no mood for company, even yours. I shall take a walk to clear my head. Give my love to Lily when you see her, and never fear, I will see that you lack for nothing, whether it be in Sydney or Sydenham."

"Oh, John," said Mary, "if only..."

"Don't say it, Mary. You will oblige me by saying nothing more on that subject. I will see you tonight and we will talk then."

And talk they did, long into the night. Mary had come from a day spent with Lily Dale, and Johnny from one spent walking the streets of London. There can be few things more dismal than this shouldering through the heedless masses who crowd every thoroughfare of the capital. There can be few things less conducive to thought than the constant stepping round mooncalves whose sole purpose in life is to clutter the pavement, the endless necessity of eluding homicidal cabdrivers, the noise and the heat and the smells and the bustle of the average London day. Yet how many of us spend every day of our lives thus, and how few ever get as far as thought at all?

Chapter Twenty-Seven

A PIECE OF PAPER

The following morning struck Lily as depressingly normal. After the previous day's news, she felt that somehow the world should have changed, that the sky, the weather, the air itself should show the difference. All her life, Johnny Eames had been somewhere on the horizon, useful or otherwise, wanted or unwanted, he had always been somewhere in her world, he had always been there to turn to. Those turnings had often been faute de mieux, but even such turnings have their comfort, and their charm. The thought of him on the far side of the world, effectively wiped from existence, left her feeling strangely lost. That there should be nothing to do this morning but walk in the park and visit the dressmakers seemed somehow inappropriate. But, appropriate or not, the morning passed, and after lunch, too, there was nothing to do but continue to pretend that the day was normal.

It was not a visitors day, so Lily was endeavouring to console her mind with darning when Mr. Eames was announced.

He was less forward, much more diffident than

of late, almost, in fact, the old hobbledehoy of their childhood.

"I have disturbed you," he said. "I am sorry, I did not realise you were all alone. I had better go."

"I am always pleased to see you," Lily replied, "and happy to be disturbed at such a task. I will ring for tea. And, you know, John, that we are such old friends that there can be nothing objectionable in our being alone together."

"That of course, is just it," said Johnny, "But one must take what one can get in this life. I am always pleased to see you, no matter what."

Having spoken thus, he sat down, and apparently devoted himself to a close and detailed scrutiny of the pattern of the carpet.

Out of the full heart the mouth speaks, or so the proverb would have it. But its application must be only to those hearts which are moderately full. Certainly few could be fuller than the two which beat the London air that afternoon, but their owners found it strangely difficult to find words. After a few meaningless exchanges about the weather and mutual acquaintances, a silence fell, and both sat mum, staring, Lily at the fire and Johnny at the carpet.

"And is it true ?" asked Lily, plucking up courage at last. "Is it true that you are to go to Australia and we will see no more of you?"

"It may well be true," said Johnny. "Likely enough it will be. It appears that it is either that or oblivion. Mr. Palliser has suggested that at some indeterminate time in the future there might be a seat in parliament for me, but I know just how much such a suggestion is worth. I have no doubt he means it sincerely, but he is a politician, and he is not the head of his party. Politics and expediency are strangely close to each other these days, and today's gratitude cannot be counted on tomorrow. The antipodes I suppose it must be, and a new life among new people."

"But surely you will have Mary to keep you company?"

"Mary will do well enough back in Guestwick. At least I can see that she will want for nothing. I could not ask her to come with me to the far side of the world. I could not ask that of anyone."

Silence fell again. The shadows lengthened, and the tea grew cold.

"Lily," Johnny said at last. "If I ask you a question, will you answer it truly?"

"I always answer you truly, John, you know that."

"Grace told me that last night you were out of sorts. She said you spent the whole evening staring at the fire and playing with a book on your lap. You started to tear a page out of it but stopped halfway. Lily, you once told me that you would write four words in your commonplace book, and when I begged to be allowed to tear them out you said it would never be. Was it that book? Is it that book you have beside you now?"

She made no answer. For a long, long, moment she was still. Then she held out the book to his waiting hand. He opened it and read on the flyleaf, torn halfway through, the four words.

"Lily Dale, Old Maid."

Their eyes met. He held her with his gaze, and, taking courage at last, ripped the page from the book.

At this point a ring at the doorbell was heard and voices in the hallway, followed by the entry of the servant.

"A message for Mr. Eames, Miss. Urgent it says." And the salver was proffered with an envelope.

They both sat back, while Johnny must of necessity take the packet.

"Excuse me," he said, and opened the seal. The perusal took but a little while, and seemed to give him no great pleasure before he refolded the paper and put it in his pocket.

"No reply," he said, and sat staring at the floor while the servant departed.

"You seem strangely downcast," said Lily. "I hope it was not bad news."

"Not exactly bad news. There are some who would call it the best news in the world, but I find I care nothing for it. It is the reward for my labours with Mr. Palliser, the little recognition that all my friends have been promising me this long while. Such a great thing it is. I am not to go to New South Wales. My post there is to be filled by Sir Raffle, who has declined the appointment which is now offered to me. There is to be a new Decimal Currency Board, and I am to be chairman. And in view of this and my past efforts, Her Majesty has seen fit to include my name in the list of Knights Bachelor."

"Oh, but this is marvellous news!", cried Lily. "Only think of it! Sir John Eames! What will Bell say when I tell her? And this new position must make your fortune too."

"It is two thousand a year and most of the work done by others. That is the way these things go. But neither the money nor the title gives me any pleasure. Indeed, there is a cruel irony to my ears in the title of knight bachelor, as you should know, Lily. I am like to live up to it in every sense. Unless....unless...no, it cannot be. I know you have twice refused to become Mrs. Eames, and I cannot think that the prospect of being Lady Eames instead would make any difference."

"You are quite right Lady Eames and Mrs. Eames would be all one to me."

"I must go."

And he made to rise, still clutching the scrap of paper with the four offending words.

But her hand upon his arm prevented him. With her other hand she tore the paper from his grip and flung it in the fire.

"Johnny," she said. "Dearest Johnny. How can you think that I would hold a trumpery title dearer than the best, the truest man in the world? For I know that is what you are, and that all my friends have been right these long years and I have been wrong. A foolish girl's pride kept her from knowing her own happiness, but say it is not too late to undo the mistake."

His heart was too full for words, but their arms were round each other's waists and no more words were needed.

Chapter Twenty-Eight

EPILOGUE

When Doctor Crofts returned that evening he found them still sitting there. He, too, needed no words. The look on their two faces said all that was needed. But words have their uses, after all, and by then it was necessary that some should be said. No-one present was a famous orator, still less a poet, and though words could never be adequate to express their feelings, they did suffice to convey the sense of what had previously been tacit. Before Johnny left the house it had been settled that all their friends should be informed as soon as might be.

"Well," said Arabella Dale, when her husband passed over Lily's letter to him, "I can't say I am overjoyed that a cousin of yours is going to throw herself away on a government clerk. I never liked that Mr. Eames, and I can't see what Lily Dale sees in him. We shall have to put up with them, I guess."

"We shall do rather more than that." said Bernard. "They must be married from Allington, of course, and it will be the best day the old place has seen for a long time. Dear old Johnny Eames has got his reward at last. It seems that wonders will never cease."

"Well," said Mr. Plantagenet Palliser, "Mr. Eames is to marry Miss Dale. I can't say that I ever noticed much of that sort of thing between them. He is a sterling fellow, and might have done much better for himself. But there is nothing against the girl, and I dare say she will try to be a help to him."

"Plantagenet, you goose," was Lady Glencora's reply. "You wouldn't notice 'that sort of thing' if it went on under your nose, which it did, as it happens. I noticed, and I did my best to help it along, so of course I am gratified at my success."

"Well," said the bishop, when he heard the news, " dear Grace has always been fond of Miss Dale, and she was a delightful guest when she was here. It will be a pleasure to welcome her into the family now that she is to be, in some sense, a cousin after all. Young Eames is a sound fellow, you know, and a rising man. They are sure to do well."

So it was to the approbation of all their real friends, and the distress of several counterfeit ones that, at very long last, Allington saw the wedding of Sir John Eames and Miss Lily Dale. I will not record the reactions of the Hon. Claudia or of Mr. Crosbie, although they did not, as Siph Dunn predicted, run off together out of spite. The day was as fine as anyone could wish, and the assembled villagers were out of their minds with amazement. That Miss Dale should be a lady was only natural. But little Johnny Eames now Sir John, and a big man in the government too, with all those lords and ministers and such at his wedding! It was truly a wonder beyond all wonders, and something they would talk of for many long years.

And many long years is what we must all now wish the happy couple. Many long years of happiness, with all the good things that life can hold. None but the brave deserve the fair, so goes the old saying. If our hero had not been exactly brave, then neither had our heroine been in all respects fair. As to the deserts in the question, dear reader, you must work that out for yourself, for further guidance you will find none. On the steps of Allington church we must leave them, on the way to their wedding breakfast, on a glorious summer morning, in the village where they grew up, surrounded by their friends, with, at last, their hearts desire.

In fiction or in life, can there be a better way to end?